Passion in the Peak

by the same author

Superintendent Kenworthy novels

THE HOBBEMA PROSPECT
CORRIDORS OF GUILT
THE ASKING PRICE
THE SUNSET LAW
THE GREEN FRONTIER
SURRENDER VALUE
PLAYGROUND OF DEATH
THE ANATHEMA STONE
SOME RUN CROOKED
NO BIRDS SANG
HANGMAN'S TIDE
DEATH IN MIDWINTER
DEATH OF AN ALDERMAN

Inspector Brunt novels

THE QUIET STRANGER
MR FRED
DEAD-NETTLE
GAMEKEEPER'S GALLOWS
RESCUE FROM THE ROSE

non-fiction

THE LANGUAGE LABORATORY IN SCHOOL
LANGUAGE TEACHING: A SYSTEMS APPROACH

JOHN BUXTON HILTON

Passion in the Peak

A Superintendent Kenworthy novel

St. Martin's Press
New York

Library of Congress Cataloging in Publication Data

Hilton, John Buxton.
    Passion in the peak.

    I. Title.
PR6058.I5P3   1985   823'.914   85-11817
ISBN 0-312-59781-9

First published in Great Britain by William Collins Sons & Co. Ltd.

First U.S. Edition

10   9   8   7   6   5   4   3   2   1

Passion in the Peak

CHAPTER 1

A March gale funnelled up the limestone dale. Rain beat against the window. Water from a leaking gutter was pouring somewhere into a bucket. Behind the storm a more pretentious wailing persisted. Nall looked up from the sheet of lavender notepaper.

'They call that bloody music?'

'Prelude for reeds and synthesizer,' Kershaw told him. 'God made the world in six days and Szolnok's been rehearsing the overture for five weeks.'

'Sounds to me as if they're still tuning up.'

'You have an uncultivated ear, Sergeant. You're a musical peasant. This is quarter-tone stuff. It's a matter of tonal education.'

'You've been here too long, Freddy. I'll have you back in the division next week.'

A dissonance petered out. The rain was sheeting horizontally across the Square.

'They must have played a wrong note,' Detective-Constable Kershaw said. 'He'll be cursing them up hill and down dale. I think he learned his English off a lavatory wall.'

'I'd rather have the crap my daughter listens to.'

'Oh, there's no lack of pop. Groups in the intermissions. Choruses of Nazarenes, Galileans and proselytes.'

'No need to be rude. Gadarenes—that's more like it.'

'You're not with it, Sarge. This is the apotheosis of the arts, an amalgam of æsthetic experience.' Kershaw was quoting from the promotional handout.

'Experiment in æsthetic bastardy. What they need's a male voice choir.' Detective-Sergeant Nall fancied himself as a baritone. He did not lack volume.

'They've got that, too. Prelude to Act Seven: Roman soldiers in the Prætorium.' Kershaw went into another heavy quote. 'Librettists and composers, choreographers and scenic artists have enshrined in the opus every form of expression to which creative man has ever aspired.'

'I wonder they haven't offered you a part.'

'They have: Simon of Cyrene. Don't you think I should take it on? You told me to work my way behind the scenes.'

'You've been here too bloody long, Freddy. And you're putting on weight, too. This country chuck'll be the ruin of you. And from what I saw in the kitchen just now, grub's not your only temptation.'

'He's wasting his time looking at her,' Sergeant Wardle said, burly and misanthropic, half out of uniform in his own home, the nearest approach the village had to a police station. 'She has ideas above a policeman, has that one.'

'Well, maybe it's time I did call him in then, before she breaks his heart. I'd hoick him with me here and now, if it hadn't been for this.'

He fingered the sheet of lavender-coloured notepaper.

'You've been here long enough to have sneaked a look at a lot of people's handwriting. Whose is it?'

Kershaw read the letter, sniffed it, held it up to the light.

'Same hand as the others,' he said.

'Clever bugger! You've been here three weeks, and the only charge you've turned in so far is an old age pensioner for pinching eggs. Not to speak of spending one whole day trying to nail a Peeping Tom rap on to a laddie who's had a nervous breakdown. I'm beginning to jump out of my skin any time anyone mentions Peak Low. Before this shower descended, we didn't hear of the place once in ten years.'

The triplet villages of Peak Dale, Peak Forest and Peak Low lie a few miles apart in a crease of the Pennines, straddling the cleft that the Midland Railway navigators drove up Great Rocks Dale to Chapel-en-le-Frith. Of the three, Peak Low is the least heard of, the least trafficked over. Its couple of hundred or so able-bodied males mostly live by tearing rock out of quarries. A few wrest subsistence of a kind from the thin topsoil, helped by a handful of wandering sheep. One or two of the cottagers brew cups of tea for hill-walkers in season. Before the year of Furnival's *Passion*, the place had known few crimes graver than unlighted bicycles and the community had been left to settle their Saturday night differences for themselves. Sergeant Wardle was in sight of retirement. He had lost such taste for trouble as he had ever had.

Then the CID had started hearing of the place. There had been pilfering of a rather more than casual order: shovels, wheelbarrows and gumboots from the building site. A subcontractor's shed had been broken into, then The Devonshire Arms. The Peakrels themselves had been affected. A Peeping Tom had explored the possibilities of the women's dressing-rooms. A village youth had borrowed a lady 'cellist's moped. Kershaw had had to pay so many visits that the DI had put him in the village on semi-permanent detachment.

Perhaps Furnival's title had had something to do with it. Perhaps DI Fewter felt challenged by Cantrell, Furnival's security officer. Perhaps he even thought that these violet denunciations were worth looking into in their own right. Certainly someone seemed to have it in for Mary Magdalene.

'This time we're to stop her from going out with Larner on Saturday night. It's Saturday today.'

Two weeks ago the press had received a warning on anonymous mauve paper that someone was going to interfere with Mary Magdalene's shoes. The editor had been public-spirited enough to pass it on to the County police, though that had not stopped him from squeezing the last drop of journalistic juices from the possibilities. The joke had been an old one, screwing the soles down to the dressing-room floor while she was on set. The Crazy Gang were generally credited with having originated that one. Whether or not, they'd had one of these notes in Buxton police station and the thing had happened.

Then there had been the bitter drink. Madge Oldroyd, who was playing the Magdalene, was suffering from a dry throat. There was a jug of barley water kept for her in the wings, and somebody had tampered with it. It was worse than nasty, it was emetic, as Miss Oldroyd had demonstrated to the assembled company. Ipecacuanha, probably—but at this stage no one thought of keeping it for analysis. The incident had, however, been forecast on lavender paper. And this time a press photographer had been waiting in the wings.

It had to be admitted that Madge Oldroyd was different. For all the talk of æsthetic amalgam, the accent did seem to be on rock, jazz and folk. And Madge was a straight— and strait—singer. She was a contralto Yorkshire lass, had risen through provincial Festivals to concert class, and nowadays went about the North Country as a professional soloist with amateur *Messiahs, Creations* and *Dreams of Gerontius*. The similarity to Kathleen Ferrier's early years did not need to be pointed and clearly it was uppermost in a lot of minds that the *Passion* would be the making of her.

She would not have been everybody's choice as Mary Magdalene. No one looking at her could believe very vividly in her sinful past. But she was struggling all the time to show that there was nothing toffee-nosed about her, and she seemed to get a kick out of decking herself out as a New Testament floozie. She was quite unlike the show-business folk about her, though anxious to be on equal terms with them all. But there was clearly someone with whom this did not work; someone was always hiding her properties just before she needed them on stage. Then there was the business of the flowers that had been waiting for her in the wings, after the cast had heard her sing for the first time the hit that they were hyping for her: *I walked the streets.*

A massive bouquet from an unnamed admirer had been delivered by Interflora. But when she got it back into her room, the whole lot withered immediately the Cellophane was taken off—not only died, unnaturally, before her eyes, but stank abominably. That morning the writer on lavender paper had warned that something was being cooked up for her, but had not said what.

There had been no warning about the final outrage. Somebody had somehow got at one of her dresses, unpicking stitches, undermining press-studs, hooks and eyes, so that the thing had sprung apart just as she was standing up from washing Wayne Larner's feet. No one would have guessed that she had such a spotty, eczematous back. It was too much for Madge Oldroyd. She walked out on the *Passion,* and a temporary Mary Magdalene had to be found— the very girl that Nall had just been teasing Freddy Kershaw about: Joan Culver. Joan was a member of the Peak Low church choir, with a sweet but not very powerful voice, who, like many others in the village, had suddenly become besotted by the stage, and was happy to act as stand-in so that Wayne Larner could learn his cues and movements.

Sergeant Nall yawned.

'Your bit of homework, Freddy, is to find out who's been writing these things. Me, I shall be watching *Grandstand.* And I'm going to have shrimps for my tea. Then I'm coming out for a night on Peak Low ale.'

He spoke as if it were a threat.

'By which time you'll know the answer. Or I shall have to forgo my ale and take over from you. And if that happens you'll be eating in the canteen next week.'

Wardle cleared his vocal cords. 'All for what? Before they're much older they'll wish they'd faced the facts and buggered off. Fancy putting on an Easter open air show in these parts!'

But Kershaw continued to play at being loyal to the cause.

'Easter's only a try-out—a dress rehearsal. Then six weeks' grafting and patching—and they speak with tongues at Pentecost.'

'Furnival's got more faith in a Derbyshire Spring than I have.'

'The theatre has a sliding roof.'

'It'll only need to slide one bloody way. The man's a nutter.'

'He can afford to be.'

A well-heeled, left of centre dilettante, Lord Furnival had conceived the notion of turning Peak Low into an evangelical Oberammergau of the Pennines. He had attracted money to the venture, had formed and headed a consortium, had even dug out a Peak Low variant of the Great Plague story —or had had one ghosted. Why should neighbouring Eyam have cornered all the germs? Hoteliers in Buxton, Bakewell and Matlock had set up a joint booking office. American agencies were fighting for seats and beds.

'He stands to lose a packet.'

'He'll be satisfied if he breaks even. His loss margin is the price he's gladly paying for doing his thing. And some people are going to make a bomb, even if the whole thing flops: coach operators, caterers. They say provisional bookings from the Mothers' Union alone are enough to pay his clerical overheads. What he's going to charge for car parking will keep the orchestra in bread. Recording royalties, TV rights, video—and he is providing employment for all these bloody poets, musicians, ballet dancers, Lesbians and consenting males. It's all talent that might never have found a taker. Mediæval patrons had the same feeling when they commissioned the odd cathedral.'

'Freddy—you've got it as bad as Furnival has.'

'You told me to get under the skin. And look what he's done for the locals.'

'Taught them that crime might possibly pay. And that's what you're here for—not to stuff yourself with Yorkshire pudding and besport yourself with the original Bakewell tart.'

Crude, uncalled for: but Kershaw knew when not to rise to his Sergeant's cloddish humours.

'You've no creative urge, Sarge,' was all he said.

Hajek, the polyglot Central European co-ordinating producer, had brought in locals for the crowd scenes, some with minor speaking parts. Men at the rock face were growing apostles' beards. Women in cottages were sewing seams to the patterns of a wardrobe mistress with an address in Paris.

'There's been more strife here about who's going to do what than the High Peak has known since the Enclosure Acts. The record of brotherly love since Furnival cut his first sod reads like the history of Christianity in the Dark Ages. Yet Furnival insists he isn't grinding a religious axe.'

'Scrupulously undenominational: a sublimation of the ecumenical spirit of our age.'

'Christ! I suppose you'll say it's not political, either. The man's a Commie.'

A Commie to Nall was anyone who believed in the welfare state. But undenominational or not, there was bland support from some churchmen and uncompromising hostility from others—including the Vicar of Peak Low, who wrote a letter to *The Times* in Ciceronian prose, deploring the prostitution of the scriptures. In his pulpit he was more specific.

'The point about Mary Magdalene is that Jesus forgave her. Neither He nor she denied her scurrilous past. *Her sins, which are many*—those were His words. Yet when I came through the woods last Thursday morning, I heard a woman singing a song whose whole point was to revel in those sins. It was the sin, not the forgiveness, that interested the song-writer. In any case, there are no sound grounds for supposing that the woman who washed Christ's feet in the seventh chapter of Luke was Mary Magdalene.'

Other opponents of the *Passion* took exception to the

playing of Christ by a pop star whose sins were also generally rumoured to have been well-rounded. But as a middle-of-the-road bishop pointed out on a chat show, theirs was essentially a religion of regeneration. And to void accusations of irreverence, the production was protected by a meticulous mystique. Larner was not to show his face to the audience. Parables and miracles were to be played out in tableaux and mime. Pronouncements and exhortations were to be sung with celestial overtones. The mind of the populace would be reflected in pseudo-folk stuff in the entr'actes. In this festival, the fringes had been granted the freedom of the apron stage: but they were rigorously selected fringes.

Nall tapped the letter again.

'Find out who's writing these. Find out this afternoon. Somewhere there must be samples of most people's writing on file. Cantrell will have access. Get it settled this afternoon, Freddy. And when you know the answer, do sod-all about it. Just tell me her name when I come out this evening—it stands out a mile that it's a woman. And next week I'll have you back to an ordinary round of honest iniquity.'

'Yes, Sergeant.'

'And Freddy—I've been wondering how you're going to tackle this.'

'So have I.'

'You're going to have to beard Cantrell. That will mean watching points.'

As professionals, they had nothing but contempt for Cantrell. It was largely by bluff that Cantrell got by, but that did not mean that he had no power: in emergencies, the Cantrells of this world can rally the forces of the Establishment.

'When I think of what might happen if you put a foot wrong with Cantrell, I'm tempted to miss *Grandstand* and do the job myself.'

But Kershaw knew that he wouldn't. Nall's idleness was as near to totality as he could get away with.

A renewed flurry beat the window. The electronic prelude soared again.

CHAPTER 2

A gust round the corner of a stone-built cottage had Kershaw pinned for a moment against a wall. Somewhere behind the storm, the orchestra achieved a primæval crescendo. It was typical of Szolnok to call them back without notice on a Saturday afternoon, like kids kept in at school.

Kershaw's gaberdine had ceased to be stormproof. As he plodded up past the pub and the school, he saw a figure crossing the storm-swept Square: a male figure, adolescent in the outgrowing-his-strength stage, round-shouldered, gangling, uncoordinated: Julian Harpur. If the afternoon had been other than it was, Kershaw might have lingered to try to find out what Harpur was doing. But who could ever answer that—least of all Julian Harpur? Kershaw had had Harpur on a short list of one at the time the Peeping Tom complaints had come in; but there had been no evidence, nothing to work on. The only thing one could do with Harpur was to make mental notes of where one saw him and what he appeared to be up to. If there was scheme and purpose in young Harpur's life, he himself seemed the last to be aware of it.

Kershaw leaned into the wind, doing his best to ignore the rain that lashed his face. Nall had not exaggerated the perils of confronting Cantrell. The man was smoothly sure of himself, would have considered it a weakness—a wetness —to sink to subtlety in any personal relationship. For all Furnival's airy æstheticism, it was an abrasive force that he had recruited to man his support lines. Cantrell was ex-army, had learned what he knew of police work as an Assistant Provost Marshal. The worst enemy that Furnival had to fight was adverse publicity. If there were hard drugs in his camp, then Cantrell's resources for rooting them out were in some ways superior to those of the police: he had access to premises. But it would not be a question of rooting things out: his job would be to dig them in. If a new bout of snide stories went the rounds about Larner, then he had to see that they stayed in the family. The Press were here in strength now, covering the practical joker angle.

Kershaw turned into the drive with its castellated lodge, the dotted follies that Furnival called owl-moperies and clod-wotteries, years ago tortured into apiarists' peacocks and squirrels, now grown out, but not quite beyond recognition.

The blonde in Reception did not want to be disturbed from a letter she was writing. Except for the orchestra, almost the entire enterprise had succumbed to the spirit of the wet weekend. But Dyer was coming down the stairs: a shaven head, burning black, close-set eyes, tight twill trousers. Dyer was Larner's agent. There were tales about Dyer's control of Larner. *Permission to fart, sir?* It was rumoured that anything that Larner did on stage had to be vetted by Dyer; that was said to be in his contract. It was Dyer who had launched Larner in the early years of Beatle-apers, had lifted him out of some sleazy group yeah-yeah-yeahing in a cellar. Dyer must have ploughed an uphill furrow, selling Larner to Furnival. There was always something going on behind Dyer's eyes. They were not on fire—but smouldering: a man reputed to be difficult. Yet face-to-face, Kershaw had never found him anything but mild and helpful.

'Looking for someone, Officer?'

'I'm going up to see Colonel Cantrell.'

Kershaw knocked on Cantrell's door and waited. Nothing happened. He knocked again and opened the door as discreetly as he could. Cantrell liked catching you out either way: for entering without being told to—or for not hearing him call. Just now he was too engrossed on the phone to expostulate.

'Well, honestly, sir, I don't know what I can be expected to do about it.'

His bony face was pink with emotional exertion, his Sandhurst moustache nicotine-stained, the white patches at either side of his bald dome clipped transparently to the skin.

'I'm not the guardian of their morals. I can't call them in like a housemaster and give them six of the best for fornication.'

He could have waved Kershaw to a chair. Kershaw, pre-empting the mood in which he meant to tackle Cantrell, sat down without waiting to be asked.

'Well—what can we expect? Of course people will say there's a shuttle-service between beds. There *is* a shuttle-service between beds. All I can say is that sooner or later you'll have to show a chosen few that they're expendable.'

Kershaw caught sight of a corner of mauve notepaper, the fourth or fifth item down in Cantrell's tray.

'Sir, I could give you a dozen names to sack, and no injustice done. I remember a similar sort of nonsense at a Divisional HQ—two staff captains in the NAAFI quarters— When you're dealing with people like this, I don't see what else you can expect. Well, no, sir, if you say so—Constable?'

'Wayne Larner, sir.'

'I know: gone to town with your girlfriend.'

The body-blow almost wrong-footed Kershaw.

'But I wouldn't let it trouble you. She looks a safe enough type to me. There's not much mischief they can get up to on a wet Saturday afternoon in Buxton, is there?'

Kershaw had to make an effort to bring his mind back to Cantrell.

'That isn't what I came to talk about, sir.'

He waited for Cantrell to volunteer something, but nothing came. He leaned forward on impulse, pinched a corner of the mauve paper and drew it from the tray.

'You've no right to do that, Kershaw.'

But then he seemed to think better of antagonizing even as menial a minion of the law as this.

'I hope you're not taking this joker seriously.'

'Aren't you, sir?'

'Good God, no. Somebody just being a bloody nuisance. Somebody who *wants* to be taken seriously. A prankster, wasting our time.'

These tricks against Mary Magdalene: had they stopped, or hadn't they, since the departure of Madge Oldroyd? There had been two incidents since Joan had been standing in. A trapdoor on the stage had suddenly fallen open while Joan was standing near it. No harm done—but if she'd been on it, she could have broken a leg. Then yesterday, just as she was crouching for the foot-washing scenario, an electrician had rushed forward from his switchboard and pulled away the microphone concealed under her bowl. Apparently he had spotted a frayed cable, and thought that the thing might have become live: only *might*.

No lavender warning of either of these events. They might have been simply stage accidents—the sort of thing that was being narrowly avoided all day long at rehearsal.

Again, Kershaw dragged himself back to Cantrell's presence.

'You hadn't thought of referring this to us, sir?'

'If we had, would they have sent you?'

Cantrell smiled a snotty smile. Kershaw kept his temper.

'It would help to know who's sending them,' he said. 'You must have a lot of handwriting in your personnel files—on their application forms and so on. Have you checked?'

'Do you know how long my working day is already, Constable Kershaw?'

Kershaw glanced at the calligraphy, though he knew all its characteristics without having to remind himself: fussy, inelegant flourishes, superfluous underlinings, a curiously stilted phraseology.

'We, on the other hand, have to take everything seriously.'

'Meaning that you're belly-aching to turn this place up-side down?'

'We would be discreet, sir. The consequences—'

'Nothing doing, Kershaw.'

'This thing *has* come down from my DI, sir.'

'Tell him that I accept full responsibility.'

'That might not impress him, sir.'

Kershaw knew that this might be more than Cantrell would stand for. He saw the colonel stiffen in his chair—but a mild voice from the door punctured his rising fury.

'Why don't you tell him, Charles? His interests might not run counter to ours. Let him see that we've been able to do a bit of detection on our own account.'

Kershaw liked Furnival. It was by being liked by people that Furnival achieved what he did. He gave the impression that he, too, liked people. Kershaw was relieved to see him.

'The point is, Kershaw, we think we know who's been writing these things. And incidentally, we've got rid of her for the afternoon. I've sent her to Manchester to do some quite unnecessary checking in the John Rylands Library. At least, she's off our necks for the next few hours. So let's go and take a peep at her pad, shall we? I'm sure it would be better for us to have an official witness.'

Kershaw was dubious. Turning over a room in the absence of its tenant might strike the DI either way—according to the outcome. But he followed the pair along the hair-carpeted corridors of the residential wing. And there was laughter behind some of the doors. One stood ajar, and they saw two men bending over a model of a stage-set. A soprano was practising a recitative. Through a landing window they could see the rain, still sheeting across the landscape like the tracks of arrows.

Cantrell had a pass-key and let them into a small bedsitter: cheap contemporary furniture, enough for reasonable comfort: a divan bed, a bedside table with a small built-in bookcase, a let-down desk that ran the length of the window. A skirt, fresh from the cleaners, lay over a chair. But there was little to point to the persona of the resident—the room looked more like a showcase for Larner. Mounted about the walls were a dozen unframed photographs of the singer: Larner in scuffed denims in his hippy period, his mouth wide open in front of a group who looked as if they regularly slept rough; Larner with a long string of pebble beads dangling over a sack-like shift; a still of Larner from a TV commercial for vermouth. Four of the portraits were autographed, and one could trace a progression. *Ricarda Mommsen, Sincerely Yours, Wayne Larner*, later *Ricky with love from Wayne*. The sleeve of a recent LP was prominent, released to warm the public for his come-back: *Fringe of Soul*. The lid of a music centre was open, and there was a cassette in place.

'I thought it was all over between those two,' Furnival said. 'Hasn't she been seen in company with a man?'

'A right monkey of a man, too, by all reports. But when is a thing all over in a woman's mind? It's all over as far as Larner's concerned. It's the detective's girl he's after now.'

'Oh—I thought he was stealing side-glances at Martha.'

'That came to nothing, sir. He's had a go at Jairus's daughter since then. I happened to stroll past at rehearsal and saw the way they were playing the scene. It did not look as if either of them could wait to get back to the dressing-room. I had a word with Hajek about it. Since then he's made a pass at the third angel from the left in the *Prologue in Heaven*. I suppose we've got to expect this sort of thing. These people have no standards.'

'You're prejudiced, Charles. Believe that if you like, but don't let your eyes stray off them. These hills and woods will be swarming with drop-outs when the show opens—but it's pious cash that buys seats in the stalls.'

Cantrell grasped at a straw of achievement.

'Well, at least, we're still keeping him off the road, sir.'

Larner had a hairy record in souped-up cars and a clause in his contract kept him away from the wheel for the duration of the show. The concession was said to have cost Furnival ten thousand. And Dyer was said to have shared his relief.

Furnival shrugged, unimpressed. He went casually across and switched on the cassette. Larner's voice hit the room, the volume turned up to its traumatic maximum. Larner's was a steel wool tenor with pleading overtones. Dyer had once marketed it as *sex in the groove*. Mercifully for the *Passion*, the phrase had not clung in the public consciousness. The jangle of guitars set Ricarda Mommsen's tooth-glass rattling on its glass shelf. A twelve-bar blues:

Once there was a garden, couldst thou not wait one hour?

'Soul in Gethsemane. I could have that young man for breach of contract. These lyrics are strictly classified material until the previews.'

Furnival and Cantrell began to look cursorily over Miss Mommsen's belongings. And in all conscience, she did not own much—three or four changes of unadventurous underwear, a few bits and pieces of cosmetics and a handful of books, about half of them in German. In a drawer of her bedside table was a compendium of lavender notepaper with rococo-lined envelopes. The first sheet had been started: 'Peak Low' and a date four days ago. 'Dear Sir—' and nothing more. The handwriting—neurotic flourishes, too pinched-up for elegance—was already familiar to Kershaw.

'Mind if I take a sheet, sir?'

'I don't see why not. Much good may it do you!'

Kershaw carefully extracted one, folded it and put it away in his wallet. He also helped himself, largely as a show of professional activity, to a spent match-end from the ashtray —one torn from a book, and advertising, of all things, a hotel in Doncaster.

'Who is she, sir?'

'Jewess. Three-quarters. The family had enough money to get out of Augsburg before the holocaust. She's a world authority on Hebrew costume, knick-knacks, environment. She's my chief research assistant.'

'Attractive?'

Furnival and Cantrell looked at each other.

'You must have heard the tales about Larner. She's thirty-four, looks forty-eight, wears brogues like horse-troughs. Some people's notions of Jews are based on a hideous caricature. Ricky Mommsen, I'm afraid, is that caricature in the flesh. And that is *not* a racist remark. Yet according to rumour, she has already found herself a new friend—odd bod though he appears to be.'

Cantrell sniggered. There were unsavoury stories told about Larner and women. There had been one loathsome episode that had been kept from the public ear and that was no more than a subject for speculation, even among those who considered themselves well informed. It was shortly after that that Larner had cut himself loose from Dyer— only to find himself out in the cold for a decade. He was said to have a gargantuan sexual hunger, with no shortage of women queuing up to keep that wolf from his door. Adolescents screamed orgiastically over the footlights. He made obscene gestures at thirteen-years-olds with his guitar. But his amorous diet was not above hags and freaks. He was a man, it seemed, of unsavoury tastes. There were tales of provincial hotels, in the early years of his one-night stands, where he was supposed to have taken cripples to his bed. Nottingham was frequently mentioned as the scene of one of his most nauseating aberrations, but there were too many versions of the story for any of them to be relied on.

And now he was out for the afternoon with Joan Culver—

'Have you seen all you want to see, Constable?'

There was nothing for it but the long, cold walk back to his billet. One sheet of uninformative notepaper, one spent match from Doncaster. It was to be hoped that Nall's ale suited him tonight.

And what had got into Joan?

Things between Freddy Kershaw and his billetor's daughter scarcely amounted to an understanding. He had taken her out twice: one evening for a pub snack, and once to see Mike Harding at the Buxton Opera House. He thought he was taking a chance there, that she might be offended by the comic's happy vulgarity. But she had laughed at cracks that he had not expected her to understand. He took her for an old-fashioned girl, and had said that to her once.

'Well, if that's what you think,' she had said, 'you might be in for a big surprise one day.'

When spring was a reality, and the footpaths had dried out, they were going to walk a dale or two together. In the local idiom, they had taken to each other. That was all there was to it. Joan was an attractive, well-built girl, twenty-fiveish, the sort of complexion you might see on a health-food poster, intelligent—had taken three A-Levels. But because of family circumstances, she had only gone on to a dead-end clerical job, and had left that when her mother died. Now she looked after her father and her unmarried brother who worked the small farm.

Freddy Kershaw could not see that Wayne Larner had any place in that ethos.

CHAPTER 3

Kershaw, wet from his walk down the hill, let himself into the cottage. Joan's father, his knees close to the fire, was watching the racing on television. He looked up apologetically.

'She'll not be late. She asked me to cook the supper. Matthew's out courting, up Beeley Moor. I reckon we'st manage all right, the pair of us.'

Then he summed up the position succinctly.

'It'll be a good job when these fancy buggers have gone home.'

Kershaw invited him to come over to the pub that evening. The old man needed no persuasion.

'Only there's no need to say too much to Joan about it, is there? A half-pint of mild'll do me no harm.'

There followed a Saturday night that was neither the brightest nor the shortest in Kershaw's recollection. Nall was pigging it on pint bitters with whisky chasers and ribbing him repetitively about Joan. And Sergeant Wardle, who joined them out of uniform, was either suffering from an unacknowledged stomach ulcer, or was determined to disseminate misery for its own sake. The Devonshire Arms was packed by some of the weirder and more clannish-minded of Furnival's retinue and it was difficult for locals to struggle to the bar. And when the policemen finally did get tankards in their hands, their elbows were pinned to their sides by Swedish clarinettists, Portuguese stage electricians and a variety of lesser contributors, including an indeterminate little man who made himself known in the lime-washed urinal.

'Prepuce—a Gentile.'

Nall was determined not to be impressed by Kershaw's report on Ricarda Mommsen.

'And you shouldn't have gone into her room, boy. Bounce from here to hell and back if she finds out about that and cares to make something of it.'

He looked askance at the Doncaster match-end.

'I don't see what that proves. Except that somebody's been to Doncaster, which isn't a crime—except against good taste and common sense.'

'I might as well chuck it away, then.'

'Unless you want it as a souvenir.'

Nall belched proudly, swallowing air between pulls at his pot, then bringing it back with a gut-rumbling crack. He had done this at short intervals every night out for years—and still thought it funny.

'So Furnival didn't seem worried? I don't think you've got the knack yet, Freddy, of reading these bloody aristocrats. When a man like his lordship smiles at you, that's the time to look out. While he's cutting your throat, he'll expect you to be shaking his hand like a pump-handle. That's what they mean by being a gentleman.'

The talk moved naturally on to Larner. It generally did whenever the subject was the *Passion*. Opinions were strong —both ways. His fans of ten years ago were overjoyed at his come-back. Others thought it nothing less than blasphemy to have cast him in the Christ part. It was a blow struck for youth and progress—that was the legend on his latest record-sleeve. In his prime he had written and sung songs about inner city emptiness. He had sat down in traffic in the cause of conservation. He had given *al fresco* concerts to feed the Third World. He had preached about his progress from reefers to the hard stuff—and his ultimate self-redemption; he had written fulminating letters to the Press about middlemen and pushers. His social conscience was touched by anything that might prink his next disc with a sparkle of gold. Some said that he had never penned a lyric in his life, that every syllable had been written by somebody in Dyer's team, that Dyer picked his causes for him and kept his engagement book free for the right demos.

But when, in the mid-'seventies, he had had to go it alone, it had not taken him long to find contracts hard to renew. He lost his touch for writing songs. His new material was thin and perfunctory. He sank down and out of the charts, was overtaken by new names, some of them sponsored by Dyer.

'It's obvious,' Nall said. 'He's both Dyer's labour and his capital. I've heard it said that Dyer's made five million to Larner's two. Without Dyer he couldn't find a bloody chord, pick his nose or wipe his arse.'

'You've got to give him some due, Sarge. He has brought something original to pop music.'

'Original? Listen: my kid's just bought his latest single. *Dawn broke my heart*. They were singing that sort of crap in the nineteen-forties. If there's anything original in a song like that, my cock's a kipper.'

'Not characteristic. A one-off sentimental. He does some-times have to put in a sop to that end of his market.'

Kershaw did not know why he was taking Larner's side. Where the hell was Larner now, and where had he taken Joan?

Wardle grunted, out of humour with everything they chose to talk about. Nall could find nothing more eloquent than another belch, which jarred up from the cavern of his belly as if it had encountered something loose on the way. He glanced over his shoulder to see what public appreciation there was for his talent. A woman with big brassy ear-rings and a half-length fur coat pulled at a black cheroot and shuddered.

That was the sort of evening that it was. And to make it worse, old Culver did not limit himself to his half-pint but, off the hook for the first time since some unspecified illness of the winter, got in a corner with some of his cronies and wound up serenely and incapably drunk. Kershaw had to manhandle him home, undress him on his bed and hunt round for a receptacle, which he dearly hoped the old man would not need. He also hoped that he would be sufficiently sprightly in the morning for Joan not to have to probe too deeply.

It was now late—and Joan had not come home. Kershaw sat up to watch the late-night film, but kept nodding and waking until he lost grip of the story. He switched off and went upstairs, was half-undressed when he heard the late private buses from town arrive with their reliefs in convoy. Many of the company were without their own transport, and Furnival was good about the trivia of welfare.

They slewed round almost under his window. He moved the curtain an inch to look down at the crowd: stage-hands, extras, box-office computer programers: French, Pakistani, Latin American, unidentified Balkan. A man in a long black overcoat and homburg was carrying a banjo-case as if it were his sole possession. One youth was dressed for the American frontier. There were couples who could hardly wait to get each other into bed—shoals of lank hair dangling over damp duffel shoulders. Some were solitary travellers: a middle-aged woman had a psychedelic plastic bag containing her boutique acquisitions of the afternoon. A sallow æsthete, lantern-jawed, was lost in reverie, illusion or void.

The man with the banjo-case was hanging about as if for some purpose, and Kershaw watched him fall in step with a short, flat-footed tubby girl who might possibly be the writer of the lavender letters. Cantrell had said that her new friend was a monkey of a man. But the disparity in their ages made it seem improbable.

And hanging about on the edge of the square, round-shouldered, emaciated and hangdog, he caught sight of that odd youth Harpur, the probable Peeping Tom, looking as if he did not belong to anyone. What the hell was he here looking for? Why was he out of his warm bed at this time of night, anyway? Did his ballast-headed parents even know he was out of the house?

As the empty coaches were pulling away, Kershaw heard another vehicle coming down from the Hall. It drove slowly across the Square, picking a careful way through the crowd: a minibus, its flank painted with crazy lettering—*The Deviants*. Who the devil were they? Another of Furnival's fringe groups?

The rain had stopped now. The puddles in the Square reflected the lights of the coaches. The pavement outside the pub shone with blobs of orange.

Joan Culver and Wayne Larner were not among those who had returned. But in any case, they wouldn't be coming by bus, would they?

CHAPTER 4

Kershaw hurled his shirt across a chair. They were old enough to know their own minds. It made him want to fetch up. He still couldn't think of this as Joan's scene.

But who the hell was he to know what was Joan's scene and what wasn't? He got into bed, nauseated by the undigested beer that was still swilling about inside him. The room twisted over when he closed his eyes, slightly to the left and backwards.

So Ricarda Mommsen was Lady Lavender; and tonight she'd told them to keep an eye on Larner and Mary Magdalene. Cantrell had spoken as if he had some sort of surveillance on Larner. Kershaw had made sure he'd got to know Cantrell's mobsters by sight. They were mostly old soldiers, looking like ex-SAS with the beginnings of middle-age spread: no telling how they would really make out in a rough-house. How subtle would they be at playing gooseberry? How effectively would they have got in Larner's way? No doubt they were dab hands at not casting their shadows over a spot of innocent philandering. Innocent? It did not seem so innocent when it was somebody you knew. And how long, Kershaw asked himself, was he going to lie here, knowing that he would have to get up and be sick sooner or later? He got up and was sick. He listened for a moment at old man Culver's door. His breathing was noisy but regular. Kershaw went back to bed and the fumes in his head drew him down into unhealthily heavy sleep. He awoke with a jerk an hour and a half later, listened sharply, knew that a car had pulled up outside. He got up and saw that it was a two-seater Lotus, parked with its headlamps full on, the engine idling—too fast and too noisy.

They were down there, under his window, Joan and

Larner, the pop-star in five or six hundred quid's worth of leather coat, his voice high-pitched and shallow, a Londoner's vowels. The beam from the car was assaulting the tower of the parish church with an unnatural brilliance. Larner opened the gate of the tiny front garden and followed Joan up the stone-flagged path to the porch. And there they stood kissing good night, outside Kershaw's line of vision, but in any case, he had no desire to see. It went on for minutes and filled him with fury. Then he heard Joan come into the house and up the stairs, treading like a hunting cat. She looked first into her father's bedroom and he heard her groan with disgust.

In the meanwhile, Larner had driven off with a bravura burst of throttle that must have wakened half the village. Kershaw heard him climb the steep hill past the school in an intermediate gear.

Then came a violent screech of brakes and tyres, a resonant crash, a tearing of metal and a thundering of falling stone. At once Kershaw had his bedside light on and was pulling on his trousers over his pyjamas. As he came out on the landing, Joan came out of her room.

'What was that?'

'Larner's car. I'm going up there. Go down and knock Sergeant Wardle up, get him to call for a squad car and an ambulance. We're going to need both. It sounded to me as if he's hit the wall up over Brackdale. It could be nasty.'

Kershaw was without official transport in Peak Low and his own car was parked in a lane, boxed in, he found, by a van. His only way up the hill had to be on foot, and he ran across the damp Square, the water splashing from the puddles. Past the school the gradient was one in six. His lungs began to burn and he had to drop his pace. The need for action had cleared the vapours from his brain. He made a note that he was physically degenerating: better start jogging next week.

Beyond the school the road rounded a hairpin bend, on

the left a sheer drop of some sixty feet where outcrop
limestone cliffs edged a rivulet at the bottom of a minor
ravine. Brackdale was one of those short, deep and bleak
little gorges in which Derbyshire specializes. And when he
rounded the bend, he saw that the crash was as bad as he'd
feared. As he advanced on it, shining his powerful torch,
something cruelly sharp stabbed into the sole of his foot,
hurting him more than he was aware of at the time. He
hopped across to the wrecked car and saw that it had been
driven into the wall on his left with an impact that must
surely have written off the engine. It had also destroyed the
wall, and the rubble thrown under the rear wheels was all
that had saved it from toppling over the edge. The bonnet,
stove in, was overhanging the gap and the vehicle was
canted up at an angle with its front wheels three feet off the
ground. There was no one in the car. It looked—absurdly
—as if Larner had got out as inconsequentially as if he had
just pulled up outside some shop. Was it possible that any
man could have escaped instant death in such a collision?
Larner must have had miraculous luck: the windscreen
had ridden up high enough to avoid the impact, and the
steering-column had lived up to its specifications and collapsed at the moment of the crash. It had to be a fluke, but
one thing was undeniable: Wayne Larner was nowhere in
sight.

   But someone else was coming now: a car on the road from
the direction of the Hall. No—not a car. A van. A police
van. Sergeant Wardle's van. Wardle must have been out on
a call. His van came to a stop, one of its tyres blowing out
like a pistol crack as he put on the brakes.

   'Blast it! By God—somebody's in trouble here!'
   'Somebody's walked out of trouble with the luck of the
devil.'
   Wardle looked into the car with his torch.
   'You mean he wasn't killed?'
   'Seems not. Incidentally, it was Wayne Larner.'

'God help us! I was out at a domestic. How they spend Saturday night in Peak Forest. Chap with his head out of the window, screaming into the street because his wife wouldn't let him have it.'

Wardle blew out his cheeks. Kershaw waited. The initiative was out of his hands now. Rank apart, this was uniform work. Then Joan came up the hill, her breathing taxed, her understanding of events confused.

'Mrs Wardle's doing the phoning.'

'I'll go down the hill,' Wardle said, 'and stop anyone coming up. After that racket, half Peak Low will be up brewing tea, and we don't want sightseers. You stay here. Guard this evidence like you've never guarded anything in your life before. Don't lay a finger on a panel of that car. And don't move your feet in the mud more than you have to. Bugger it!'

He too had stepped on something jaggedly sharp. He pulled out of one of his shoes a vicious iron spike, a sort of three-dimensional letter Z, its shank about three inches long.

'The road's littered with them. We had these in the war —at least, Jerry had. In Normandy. Chucked them behind their retreat. Whichever way they fall to the ground, one sharp end has to stick up. Mind where you tread, lad.'

Wardle walked off, exploring the ground with his disc of light before each step. Kershaw heard him snap at some Peak Lowite who was already half way up the hill.

'And I'm telling you, free country or no bloody free country, I'm not having that road trodden any more than it needs to be trodden. One man's foot could destroy evidence that matters.'

Left to themselves, Joan was short-tempered with Kershaw.

'Aren't you going to look for him? Wayne! Wayne!'

She shouted desperately, but her voice was lost against the backcloth of night and the ravine.

'Are you just going to stand there and do nothing?'

'There's nothing we can do until help comes. Sergeant Wardle was right. I have to guard this spot.'

Then he heard something, or thought he did. Was it a human sound, down there, at the bottom of the chasm? He could not be sure. If it had come at all, it did not come again. It had been too faint for him to be really sure that he was not mistaken. But if it had been anything at all, it had been a woman's cry.

He went to the edge, tried to shine his beam down, could see no farther than the branches of the trees that fringed this part of the cliff-top. And was that a car he heard, higher up the hill—or wasn't it? The night was too wild to be sure of anything. In any case there were cars on the move about the Hall half the night. These people never seemed to sleep.

'Larner! Larner! Are you down there?'

No answer. He had surely been mistaken. How long was it going to take assistance to get here? It depended where the mobiles were, what they had on at this time of night. He shone his torch inside the car and something caught Joan's eye.

'My bag! I left it behind.'

It was in the glove compartment on the passenger side: a small brocaded cosmetic bag.

'I'll get it for you.'

'For goodness' sake be careful.'

Kershaw put his hand to the handle of the car door. And his simple touch was enough to do what gravity had not quite managed unaided. It set the car moving. It dislodged the keystone that was not very securely jammed under the rear wheel.

He had to jump aside to avoid being pushed over the ravine himself. The car richocheted from one tree-trunk to another. For one hopeful moment it looked as if it might be stopped from going the whole way. But then it found a gap, slithered through it, began to somersault. Nothing could

prevent it now from going right to the bottom. And now
came what was beyond doubt a woman's cry—a cry that
became a strangled scream—and was then extinguished.

CHAPTER 5

Sunday morning—Kershaw's third in Peak Low. The first
two had been glorious days of unbuttoned leisure: the crime
wave that had brought him here in the first instance had
not been all that demanding. There had been time to dawdle
through the Sunday papers, to exchange righteous indignation with old Culver about the state of the world; time to
sit in the kitchen and natter to Joan while she cooked the
dinner. Today's contrast was too sickening to countenance.

For one thing, he had been up most of the night, most of
it writing a report that appalled him when he woke up and
remembered it. He had not finally fallen asleep until about
five, and then it had been the sort of sleep that came
inexorably over creeping flesh, closing heavy lids beyond
resistance.

He woke again about seven, heavy and unrested—and
that was because of the noise in the Square. A convoy of
police vehicles had formed themselves into a mobile HQ:
wireless vans, pick-ups, motorcyclists. Fewter, the DI, was
talking to Nall. The pair of them drove together up the hill.

Kershaw dressed hurriedly and went across in search of
information. There was none, other than that they were
hoping to get some heavy lifting gear down to the car by
some means. And a cross-country search for Larner was
being mounted in an outwards-moving circle from the
grounds of the Hall.

Kershaw went back indoors to wash and shave. Old
Culver was on the landing, on his way to or from the
lavatory.

'By Gad, that was some night out!'

He was unaware that anything had happened—unaware
to the point of sounding stupid.

'Joan won't be up yet, I suppose. She must have been
very late in. Was she?'

'I don't know,' Kershaw said. 'There was an accident. I
don't know yet what's happened.'

He did not want to talk until he knew something. When
the car had crashed and the woman screamed, he had
wanted to be down there, at the bottom of the ravine, doing
something. But there was a huge gap in the wall now, and
the road was still scattered with the foul spikes. If any more
vehicles passed, if any more tyres blew out on this hairpin,
then chaos was going to be multiplied. If a police car was
immobilized, nobody would be able to get anything done.
Yet down there, since the scream, there had been only
silence, except for the splashing of the water at the bottom
of the gulf. To think of climbing down the cliff-face would
be madness. That was a job for professional mountaineers
—and by daylight. There were valley-bottom ways into the
cleft, both upstream and downstream, but Kershaw was not
familiar enough with this tract of countryside to risk looking
for them in the dark. And it would be useless for the mobile
to arrive while he was a mile away trying to sort out sodden
footpaths.

A dislodged boulder had been hanging precariously since
the car had fallen. Now it started to slither again. Kershaw
heard it gather speed, strike a tree, then plunge, bouncing
off metal as it landed.

Dicky Morgan and Bill Chaplin were the first to arrive
in their Panda, cool and as yet not fully believing. It was
normal to arrive in a place and find that a report amounted
to nothing.

'Is there a field we can cross? If we can find a way in,
perhaps we can work our way down to the stream.'

Ten minutes later, Fewter and Nall came, together. Nall

was now reasonably sober and suppressing nausea, belching inwardly, sourly, and of necessity. And even at the best of times, it was difficult making verbal reports to Fewter. He had a genius for misunderstanding—for getting hold of the wrong end of the stick at the very beginning, then coming back to his misconceptions at frequent intervals.

'You're telling me, Kershaw, that you pushed the car over?'

'Not pushed, sir.'

'Have you been drinking, Kershaw?'

'I did have a few during the course of the evening—off duty—but—'

'You'd better get yourself indoors before any member of the general public catches sight of you. A man in your condition can only be a menace on a job like this. Go and tell Sergeant Wardle to put signs out diverting traffic round the village. And don't let me catch sight of you again tonight. I'll have a reckoning with you in the morning.'

Fewter had briefly questioned Joan Culver.

'And what light can you throw on this, young lady?'

'Only that I spent the afternoon and evening with Mr Larner. He brought me back home—and about three minutes after he left my house, we heard the crash.'

On his way to find Wardle, Kershaw escorted Joan Culver home. The rain had started again—black rain—black, it seemed, from the blackness out of which it was pouring. Joan was shivering from cold and shock. Neither could find anything to say. When he had finished helping Wardle with the road-signs, he went in and stayed downstairs, unable to sleep, straining his ears now and then for any movement in the night outside that might tell him anything. Twice he went and opened the front door, stood and listened. But there was no sound beyond the pouring rain. He turned and went indoors, and on impulse started writing his report.

It was the bare facts that he had given Fewter by word

of mouth—a condensation, but not the condensation of a man who intended missing anything out. He had been badly at fault—badly enough to ensure his dismissal from the Force—as if he ought to be concerning himself with that now! If he hadn't put his hand on that car, some unknown woman would still be alive. Why had he had to worry about that bloody handbag? Well—that was how it had happened, and he wasn't going to say otherwise. Kershaw had an antediluvian attitude to the truth. You told a lie, then had to work up a network to support it. And before you knew where you were, something had slipped that you'd overlooked, and you were in a worse hole than you'd been to begin with. And that was only a rationalization—useful if ever you felt you needed an excuse for telling the truth. Truth was truth. When in doubt, tell it.

It looked terrible on paper. He screwed up his first three efforts after only a line or two, decided that the fourth was as bad as the others, but that it had to stand. It had to be got on with, finished. Tell it how it happened.

Old Culver came downstairs in a shabby old dressing-gown.

'What's happened? What's going on out there?'

'I don't know the full story yet. I'm going over there again now, and I may not be back. They'll probably want me.'

A lot of villagers were out and about now, swanning round the perimeter of the Square as if the HQ were a travelling fair. 'They've got a body out.'

'Who?'

'A woman. They've taken her to hospital.'

Then Sergeant Nall was there too. Thank God the DI was not with him.

'Ah, Freddy. The very man. I need to make medicine with thee, my lad. Let's go over to your billet.'

As they went into the house, Joan was just coming downstairs. She pulled the kitchen door closed behind her. Kershaw took Nall into the little-used front room and pushed his statement across the table. Nall flicked it to one side. 'Just talk your way out of it, Freddy.'

'I'm not trying to talk my way out of anything.'

'Freddy—I'll grant that you have three-quarters of the brains in our office. Me, I have nine-tenths of the experience. And Fewter has rank. Fewter's not gunning for you. He wouldn't want the trouble. And nor would I. Play this quietly, and it will go away. Fewter doesn't want to lose you, and I don't want to have another rookie to train.'

Kershaw felt his self-control slipping.

'Look—for God's sake tell me: who was the woman under the car?'

'Of course, you don't know yet, do you? Ricarda Mommsen: the little Jewess who liked Larner's records. It's a good job she was wearing clothes that people recognized. We might have been a bit stumped by the rest of her. They took her off to hospital—but when you ask how she is, they only shake their heads sadly.'

'She does have some chance?'

'Chance? I don't think there's a bone in her body that isn't broken. I never cease to marvel at the human body's capacity for survival.'

Kershaw slid his statement back towards Nall. Nall smoothed it under his fingers and began to read it, cursorily at first; at least, so he tried to make it seem. Then he read a couple of paragraphs twice. 'All right,' he said at last. 'Very good. Well observed. Well put together. Nice touch of English here and there. Couldn't hope to match it. It presents a clear picture, draws intelligent conclusions. Some. As between you and me, this would do fine. But it can't possibly go forward as it is. I wouldn't even like Fewter to see it as it stands. And Gleed's coming from Derby, you know, to take charge. Gleed! That's all we need in the division, a spell of Gleed on the doorstep. If Gleed were to see this—'

'What the hell am I supposed to do with it, then?'

'Cut it down by half its length, for a start. Stick to your facts and forget your theories. And another thing—Furnival and Cantrell invited you into Miss Mommsen's room. They took on that search on their own responsibility.'

'I thought I'd made that clear.'

'Then make it twice as clear. Say it in more than one way. And this business of getting that article out of the glove compartment: that didn't happen. The car was all set to slide down of its own accord, any second.'

'Sergeant!'

'Look, Freddy—nobody's asking you to tamper with the truth. Just miss some of it out, that's all. Shift the emphasis a bit. There's no point in begging for the bullet. I know that car went down of its own accord. Fewter knows it went down of its own accord. Why the hell can't you bloody well say so?'

'I told Fewter last night how it happened.'

'Fewter took nothing in last night—not to be certain. I've told you, all Fewter wants—'

'Sergeant, I know perhaps I had a couple too many last night—'

Sergeant Nall looked at him with a ham-acted mixture of incredulity and fear.

'Well, thank God you haven't put that into writing. You were as sober as I was last night.'

'Fewter didn't seem to think so.'

'Never mind what Fewter said. I've had a word with Fewter this morning. I've told him you spent yesterday evening with me, and I'll vouch for the state you were in. The day Fewter says anything to me about drinking off duty, he knows what my comeback will be. It's putting this other stuff on paper that won't do. Look, Freddy—nobody knows—'

'You've got my statement, Sergeant. That's how it stands.'

'Freddy, I'm trying to keep you out of the mucky end. You could go places in this Force, you could.'

'I'm not doctoring what I've written.'

'Then you'll be out, lad. I can even see you on a man-slaughter rap.'

Somehow the statement had made its way to the middle of the table again. Kershaw had a sudden desire to pick the document up, to remind himself of what exactly he had said. But he resisted: he knew what he'd written.

'I don't think you've ever tried parleying with Gleed, have you?' Nall asked him.

'That's my lookout.'

'I can't give you time to think it over, Freddy. Gleed—'

'Would you like me to wait and hand it to Gleed in person?'

Nall picked up the statement, folded it, put it away in an inside pocket, stood up and remained for three seconds studying Kershaw.

'Don't you know how I feel, Sergeant?'

'Of course I know. But there's no need to jump off your branch, laddie.'

Nall turned and left him. Kershaw watched him cross the Square, his shoulders rounded.

CHAPTER 6

Fewter had got on the wrong side of Joan Culver from the very beginning. It was one of his few basic working theories that if you got your subject's back up from the start, you were more likely to unearth the natural man—or woman. Fewter came in just as Nall and Freddy were leaving. He had something to say to Freddy, something nasty, she could tell from the looks on both their faces, though she wasn't able to catch what they said. It was a pity about Freddy. She hadn't found a decent word to say to him since she had come back last night. It was partly the way that he had looked at her that had peeved her—as if he were condemning her for having gone out with Wayne. Who was Freddy Kershaw to decide who she should go out with? It had been fascinating at first, having a detective as lodger. She had never seen behind police scenes before. But it soon became a commonplace. It was true that Freddy seemed more intelligent than most of his colleagues, had read more, was altogether more thoughtful. But he was exactly like them in so many other ways. He drank too much, he smoked too much, he swore too much when he did not think she was in earshot. She did not consider herself a prude: it was just that these men were not adult.

Inspector Fewter would not take an armchair—settled himself facing her at the front-room table. She could feel what store he set by formality.

'Let's take first things first, Miss Culver. How did that car come to go over the edge?'

'I don't know,' she said. 'I didn't see.'

She owed it to Freddy to protect him on that point. If she hadn't mentioned her bag—

'You weren't looking, I suppose?'

'How could I have seen? It was a filthy dark night. There was only one light and that was Mr Kershaw's.'

'You had better be telling me the truth, Miss Culver. I want to know everything that happened yesterday. And by everything, if you are in any doubt about the meaning of the word, I mean all that took place—not just those things you consider might be important. All that happened.'

'I can't think there's much I can tell you, Inspector. Wayne asked me if I'd like to go to Buxton with him. We didn't do anything exciting, and I didn't at any time notice anything sinister.'

'Never mind what you consider sinister. What did you *do*? Where did you go? Let's begin at the beginning. Were you and Mr Larner regular friends, or did he just pick you up?'

'He did not just pick me up—though this was the first time I'd been out with him.'

'Doubtless you understand the difference. I don't.'

'I had been standing in for Mary Magdalene.'

'Ah—your big chance, I suppose?'

'I was never fool enough to think that. They needed to have somebody standing in the right place, giving the cues, until they signed up a professional. Though I admit I was thrilled to bits to be asked. But it was only because I happened to be handy and knew the scenes. I sing in one of the choruses, and when the news came that Madge Oldroyd had walked out on the show, Mr Hajek, the producer, swung round and pointed to me. "Miss I-don't-know-your-name, will you stand in for a rehearsal or two?"'

'Chance of a lifetime,' Fewter said.

'Not really. Of course, I started off with high hopes. Who wouldn't? But when I heard a playback of one of the tapes, I knew how hopeless it was.'

She did indeed: disastrous disillusion. Against the backing of the professionals, her voice was too feeble, too uncommercial, and she was shocked by her own High Peak vowels.

'At least it brought you to Larner's notice.'

'That's true.'

'And you say this was your first date with him?'

'It was.'

'He drove you out of Peak Low in his car?'

'No. He couldn't. There's a story behind that. He was not allowed to drive his car for the duration of the show, because he was supposed to be a dangerous driver. There was a clause in his contract. So he'd hired a taxi.'

Never before in her life had she enjoyed the extravagance of a taxi from Peak Low to Buxton. Half of her wanted to be seen by everybody in the village; the other half wanted to lean back invisible.

'So what did you find to do in Buxton? It was a filthy afternoon.'

'I'd a few odds and ends of shopping to do.'

A pork pie for her father, who liked them from a particular shop; some blouse buttons to match; the hope of a length of velvet from a remnant shop. There was no need to tell Fewter that Wayne had been bored to death by her shopping. And he had been obsessed about not being recognized, had worn dark glasses despite the gloom of the afternoon, to try to fool the autograph-hunters. And all he could think of was what he could buy for her—ludicrously expensive things in every other shop-window: a quartz watch, a cameo brooch, an original watercolour that she just happened to say was quite nice, even a nylon fur fun coat. She did not tell Fewter any of this: it would only give him the wrong idea. She'd thought about it—she was not quite the idiot she might look—had decided on balance that Wayne was not trying to buy her. He just wanted to give her pleasure. He wanted to give everyone pleasure. And he didn't seem to have any money sense. It was a long time since Wayne Larner had had to wait until tomorrow for anything he wanted.

What were they going to do with themselves when she'd bought the few things that she needed? There was no sign that the rain was going to abate. It was more like twilight than mid-afternoon.

'So? You did your shopping—'

'Then went to a hotel.'

'Which hotel?'

'The Badminton.'

'Ah!'

A wealth of insolence and innuendo.

'How long did you stay there?'

'Long enough to have tea.'

'Where did you have your tea?'

'I told you—in the Badminton Hotel.'

'I mean, where in the hotel?'

She paused fractionally.

'In the residents' lounge.'

She stared the Inspector out, eye to eye, challenging him to say outright that there had been more in the visit to the Badminton than that.

'And after tea?'

'After tea we went and got his car from the garage.'

'Just like that? I would have thought that they'd have been sticky about releasing it.'

'I did not hear all that was said. There was a row about it. I rather think that Wayne ended up by bribing an assistant.'

'So that he could show off to you what a daredevil driver he was?'

'As a matter of fact, I was partially responsible for persuading him to go and get the car. It didn't seem right to me that a man of his fame should be kept under a prohibition like a schoolboy under punishment.'

'So where did he drive you?'

'Into Cheshire.'

'Why Cheshire?'

'He just drove. He just loved driving.'

'And has endorsements on his licence to prove it.'

'He's a very good driver,' she said. 'Fast, it's true. And I'm not used to fast driving. But his control is superb. I thought I was going to hate it at first, but I ended up enjoying myself.'

Over the Cat and Fiddle Moors—what a drive! He broke speed limits as a matter of course, seemed utterly confident that he would not be caught. She had never before conceived of eighty-five miles an hour as a man's idea of relaxation: a certain type of man. Wayne Larner's skill and confidence communicated themselves. She ought to have been frightened by the risks that he took, but his timing, his judgement of speed and distance put him in absolute control. Style: that was what he had.

They had gone miles into Cheshire—Alderley Edge, Knutsford, had had dinner in a monumentally nineteenth-

century hotel. He had talked to her—talked to her a lot—
about his early days, his beginnings, what it was really like
to be a slave to Dyer's machine. She had the feeling, once
he had got going, that it was the truth he was telling, that
he desperately needed a chance to tell it to sympathetic ears.
She did not try to put this across to Fewter. It would be
beyond his comprehension—and was in any case irrelevant.

Over dinner, Wayne casually said that he had half promised to look in at a nightclub between Castleton and Hope,
where there was not at all a bad floor show, and he might
sing a couple of numbers. She wanted to hear him sing in
person, to be seen with him in a fashionable place as his
guest. Ten years ago he had had hundreds of thousands of
fans—but never one more eager or credulous than Joan
Culver. She looked dubiously at the clock on the dining-
room wall.

'We're a safari away from Castleton. We could never make
it in time.'

'Time? As long as we get there between midnight and
four—I'll give them a ring, let them know we are coming.'

She gave Fewter no more than the bare facts. He seemed
to think that there must have been something particularly
suspicious about going to Knutsford. That dinner had been
the zenith of middle-class respectability.

Then they had had a night ride across the plain and back
over the heights. She was agog for speed now—aglow too
with the Beni she had had with her coffee—a rare indul-
gence: as had been a Martini and three glasses of Goldener
Oktober at table. The white lines, the cats' eyes leaping at
them round smooth, fast curves, Wayne's faultless braking
at hazards seen a split second in time: it was a symphonic
fusing of the physical and the emotional, at once soothing
and exhilarating. She was aware of the reality of Wayne
Larner beside her, the charisma that had galvanized thousands. It was an ecstasy of motion at the call of a man's will.

'This nightclub near Edale—?'

'The Grey Cat.'

'Did he sing there?'

'He did.'

'And what time did you leave?'

'About half past two.'

'So what time did you get home?'

'I didn't look at my watch. I'd say between three and half past.'

Her most abiding memory at that point was the stench of stale beer vomit when she looked into her father's bedroom.

'Miss Culver, I want you to be very careful indeed about my next question. Were you under the impression at any time during your outing that you were being followed? Did Larner think that you were being followed?

'I don't think so. Except by some of Mr Cantrell's security men, his bodyguard, always on his trail. He said he had come to regard them as part of the landscape.'

She was not sure why she decided to suppress the next bit: how Wayne had tricked Cantrell's henchmen in Macclesfield. Surely Fewter was above bothering about a traffic offence? They had shot unexpectedly the wrong way down a One Way Street—and had got away with it. They had lost their tail, stuck at the red two sets of traffic-lights back.

'Did you at any stage run into anyone that Larner knew?'

'Only at the nightclub.'

'Not in Cheshire?'

'Nowhere at all in Cheshire.'

'And who did he know at The Grey Cat?'

'Only the management and the waiters—and a group called The Deviants, who were also singing there—one of the groups from the *Passion*.'

'Detective-Superintendent Gleed is on his way from Derby and will certainly want to go over all this again with you, so if there is anything you wish to alter or add, Miss Culver, it would be better not to have a completely different story to tell. Mr Gleed is not the most patient of men.'

She shook her head. Fewter left. She went back into the kitchen, asked her father what he fancied for his dinner. The very suggestion of food seemed to nauseate him—as it nauseated her. But she supposed she had better get something for Freddy and started joylessly peeling potatoes.

Joan Culver's appearance totally belied the turbulence within: that was the mistake that Freddy Kershaw had made. It was all very well looking like a 1930s advertisement for wholemeal bread, new laid eggs and malted milk drinks. Maybe she did look the perfect country girl: that was another thing that Freddy had said to her—and then wondered why it had seemed to get him off on the wrong foot.

They called the house a farm, but it had not been one for some years. Her brother Matthew had farmed less and less, and their effective income came from the irregular, unpredictable and, it always seemed to her, furtive buying and selling that he did up and down the countryside. She did not trust her brother. One of these days he was going to be in trouble.

When she had volunteered to give up her studies to housekeep for them, it had only been meant as a postponement. A marriage was supposed to be in the offing, and her sister-in-law would be taking over the chores. But that marriage did not materialize. And the woman that Matthew was 'courting' up Beeley Moor (he had not come home last night, she had not expected him to) was married and did not seem to want a divorce.

Joan Culver knew that she was caught in a domestic trap —and that there would be no escape for her unless she made it herself. She had known for some years now that hesitation was fatal—and yet she had continued to hesitate. The more Peak Low irked her, the more firmly she seemed to become entrenched. The wrong marriage would only be another trap. On sentimental—and dutiful—grounds, she hesitated to abandon her father, who if ineffectual, was at least benign.

And Peak Low held nothing for her: a mobile library, a bland and distinctly unnourishing social round in the wake of a poorly supported church. The sudden advent of the *Passion* had held out an unexpected promise of fun. And it was a coincidental irony that she had once had a juvenile crush on Wayne Larner.

She had been a Larner fan when she was thirteen. That had been in the years of his block-busting singles: *Blue Baby* and *Hole in my Heart*. Joan Culver at school had been a most biddable child. She knew now that she had been in danger of missing out on her youth simply to please her teachers. But it was pop music that bought her into the fold of her contemporaries. It was in the Third Form that she uncharacteristically found herself sharing the tastes and vaporous daydreams of some of the flightiest girls in the class: John, Paul, George and Ringo, Manfred Mann, Freddy and the Dreamers—and Wayne Larner. She suddenly found herself a popular fountain of 'knowledge' about their idols. The Third Form believed everything that the disc jockeys told them, everything they read on the record-sleeves and in the *Melody Maker*. They knew stars' birthdays and favourite foods, their drinks and pastimes. Joan's memory had always been vivid and immediate. She knew everything that Dyer wanted her to know about Wayne Larner.

She knew that he had been christened Johny Lummis and that he had had a rough childhood in London. She knew that he had learned to play his first guitar chords on an instrument he had made with his own hands in the Hobbies Class at his Comprehensive (this whole story was an *a priori* invention of Dyer's). She knew that his first public performance had been with a group that they had started while he was still at school, The Stalagmites, so-called because their first engagement had been at a far from pretentious coffee-shop called the Stalag. They were earning money from their music when they were sixteen. And it was in the Stalag that Dyer had discovered Wayne, taking him up, separating him from his friends, launching him towards the big time. His first golden disc had been *Take what I'm Showing You*. His first LP had been *Blue Groove*.

There had been a girl in Wayne Larner's life in the early days. She had been in the same form as him at school, had sung with The Stalagmites: Sue Bistort. She and Wayne had married young and she had been something of a drag on the fantasies of Joan Culver and her friends. And surely she had brought no joy to Dyer, for though she was tolerated in the Stalag, anyone could see that she had been unlaunchable anywhere else. And she was not long in disappearing from Wayne's life—though Joan and her Derbyshire friends, in common with the general public, were deprived of any detail. Larner came back from his first transatlantic trip with a Filipino. Joan and her friends admired Wayne as something more than a mere twanger of chords. He was a man who passionately *cared*, who would fight tooth and nail for things that concerned him, who could never suppress his rage at the right things to rage at. He was anti-vivisection, anti-atomic waste, anti-teacher power.

Then came his thrust for independence—and his eclipse. The Third Form was not really conscious of what was happening to him. As he slipped out of their charts, others slipped in. New performers, with new gimmicks, inflamed their enthusiasms. When the news broke that Wayne Larner was coming to Peak Low to take the Christ part, Joan had not played one of his records for years.

And it was only a passing interest that she took, something perhaps just a little stronger than mere curiosity. She knew by now how adolescent enthusiasms were manipulated. When she first spotted Wayne in the village, it was the first time she had seen him in person. He must be getting now towards the forty mark—his age was glossed over nowadays in the publicity handouts—but there was something about him that still had the power to hold. She was aware of the irony when he offered her an outing to Buxton. What would the Third Form have thought about that, if they could have foreseen it?

Never before had the Sunday cooking smelled so vile: the steam of cabbage water, the wave of heat when she shoved the Yorkshire pudding in the oven. Water boiled over from a pan of carrots, and the entry of Freddy Kershaw at that moment did not add to the sweetness of the joys of domesticity.

'I just came to let you know,' he said, 'that I can't stay to dinner.'

'Now he tells me.'

'I have to remove myself from Peak Low.'

He looked ashen; but she did not find his wretchedness endearing.

'*Remove* yourself from Peak Low?'

'I happen to serve in a force,' he said, 'where telling the inconvenient truth is not encouraged.'

That did not mean anything to her. She did not know about his statement. He went down another few points in her estimation for talking in riddles.

'You'll be in this evening, I expect—after closing time?'

'No. I'm going upstairs now to collect my things.'

Only then did she have the feeling that a phase of her life was over.

CHAPTER 7

Gleed looked at Kershaw without a smile, but with no rancour. 'Ah! George Washington the Second, demanding a hatchet job.'

Kershaw made a facial expression tantamount to acquiescence.

'Not my business,' Gleed said. 'And I don't propose to

make it mine. It's up to your Superintendent and the Chief
Constable. And I can't think there's any doubt of the outcome. Sergeant Wardle has lost no time clearing himself.
He's let it be known that he gave distinct orders for you to
leave the car alone. So I have to manage without the services
of a detective-constable who has been in this village for the
last few weeks, and who might therefore be a mine of
information about local personalities.'

Kershaw had met Gleed at County Conferences, though
his only real dealing with him had been on the Board when
his transfer to CID had come up. Gleed was a man at the
beginning of his fifties who had been in one of his strong
silent moods that day. That was his common attitude, which
left him something of a permanent enigma. The only thing
that was really known about him was his frigid efficiency.

'May I take it that nothing you have observed in Peak
Low had led you to expect last night's events?'

'Nothing, sir.'

'I'm glad to hear it. I would like to think that if there had
been anything, it would have found its way into one of your
reports.'

'There's been nothing, sir—except the letters from Miss
Mommsen and the things that have happened to two Mary
Magdalenes.'

'And you have a theory about them?'

'No, sir—except that the incidents concerning the second
Magdalene might well have been accidents.'

'Good, Kershaw. I like a man who does not theorize for
the sake of having something to say. Pity we seem so likely
to be about to lose you. I'm afraid that Inspector Fewter is
very anxious to get you out of Peak Low, and you'll understand that I cannot interfere in divisional discipline.'

'Sir.'

That was that.

*

Monday was a day that might have seemed slack to casual observers—and the Press. There was nothing to report, but like the placid swan, there was a lot going on under the surface. A massive force came under command, including dogs, helicopters, men beating heather with ash-plants, men moving in line abreast across moors and fells, men poking into caverns and dales. Relays of plainclothes women were sitting by Ricarda Mommsen's hospital bed, and the Jewess was defying prognosis by remaining alive though in a deep coma. Gleed was talking to people, treating all men alike— and detaining no one. Dyer was finding it difficult to get an interview with Furnival: he was worried that Furnival might go to another agent for Larner's replacement. But Furnival, it seemed, had no wish to discuss his intentions at the moment. There were some who believed that Larner might still show up. Others believed that he must surely have died of shock and exposure.

Julian Harpur, Peak Low's strange adolescent, whom his parents had presented to the village throughout his childhood as a genius, mooched about Peak Low and the perimeter of the theatre. And various rumours had tracked round the *Passion* Company: that Furnival was considering calling off the show; that a fringe group called The Deviants were in trouble for singing in a local club hits that were not due to be heard in public for some time yet; and that there had been an almighty row between his lordship and Cantrell. Some said that Cantrell had been told that if there was one more practical joke on or off stage, he was out. Others said that he had been carpeted because Larner had given his heavies the slip in Macclesfield. And someone even had hold of the story that Furnival had called Chief Superintendent Kenworthy out of retirement to come and sort things out.

The show had to go on, and on the Wednesday morning, Furnival and a stranger—no one knew what Kenworthy looked like—strolled into the auditorium during rehearsal.

A disturbance was taking place in the orchestra stalls. Kenworthy saw that at the centre of it was Cantrell, who had been pointed out to him, and that the security man was accompanied by two of his minions. They were evicting someone from one of the theatre seats: a young man, aged between eighteen and twenty, fleshless, round-shouldered, with eyes that looked hunted by the world and yet contemptuous of it. He had an immature moustache, sparse yet at the same time drooping, and when Cantrell ordered him to leave the theatre, he complied meekly, though with a look of hatred.

'I don't normally mind the locals dropping in at rehearsals,' Furnival said. 'It makes for good will, and we get feedback from their reactions to the script. But Cantrell needs to be seen to be doing something. I've vetoed practically everything he's suggested since Sunday morning, and he knows he's no more now than chief watchman.'

'And who's the laddie he's chivvying?'

'A village boy—Julian Harpur. His parents brought him up as a loner, telling people he had an IQ that broke all bounds: probably still believe it. But he had some accident doing an experiment at home with chemicals he had helped himself to from the school laboratory. They say something's jarred his brain: I dare say that's not the medical terminology. But it's hard to know, because even before the mishap, nobody had any rapport with him. They say he was always an oddity. At school they wanted to prosecute for theft of the chemicals. The staff couldn't stand him. Now, of course, he's unemployed—unemployable, has nothing to do but hang about thinking his own thoughts. And they don't seem to be bringing him much pleasure.'

Cantrell had moved on to a second intruder, a small man in late middle-age who had on a navy blue suit worn to a shine, and clamped squarely on his head a black homburg. He was also wearing a pair of round-lensed, tortoiseshell-framed spectacles. In fact he appeared by some miracle to have assembled all the trappings for an undiluted nineteen-thirtyish appearance. Maybe that had been his style all his life.

Unlike young Harpur, this man tried to resist ejection. Furnival and Kenworthy were not near enough to hear what he was saying, but he looked like the sort who would argue volubly that he was doing no harm, and what sort of Christianity was this that put up barriers to keep people out? But when one of Cantrell's henchmen put a hand on his shoulder he stood up to go, and picked up from between his feet a black banjo-case.

'Who?' Kenworthy asked.

'A dogsbody of one of the fringe groups. Also a friend of Ricarda Mommsen's. At least, he was often seen talking to her.'

'Have you many people about the place who are un-accounted for?'

'We try to account for everybody, but it's difficult. Not everybody is employed directly by me. Some of the groups have their own hangers-on—technicians, odd-job men—men like the one you just saw chucked out.'

The man with the banjo was leaving, turning over his shoulder with some quip that he no doubt considered the soul of wit.

At that moment a Gregorian chant rose above the light rustle of wind in the treetops outside the theatre: the *Passion* was not all jive and jangle.

No bread, no scrip, no money in our purse—

The rehearsal was about to get under way when there was yet another interruption. A couple of delivery men had arrived from somewhere with a large wooden crate, which they were carrying down the aisle from the back of the theatre.

'Where do you want this?'

The man addressed himself to Hajek, who came out with an array of abuse that would have fascinated an infantry drill sergeant. Hajek, Hungarian, an escapee from 1956, was under-endowed with patience.

'What is it, for Christ's sake?'

The man thrust at Hajek a delivery note, which the producer crumpled up and threw far from him.

'Take the bloody thing backstage—round the outside of the theatre. Why is it that everything matters here except the bloody performance?'

No bread, no scrip, no money in our purse—

A double quartet of apostles was setting out to preach on the Galilee Sabbath. They were rugged figures—and Furnival's purse ran to voices from Milan as well as the Rhondda. The composer of the sequence was sitting with the producer in the front row, in a filthy anorak, his sharp grey beard pointing to the sky in what appeared to be rhapsodic satisfaction.

This was one of those moments in rehearsal when the timing, the team-work, the faithfulness to artist's intent were going as well as most men would hope for in the final performance—except that, unguessed-at by many of the audience, the final production would be mimed to a digital recording.

Now the unaccompanied singing tapered away into four minutes of high comedy. Yet it was sympathetic—even reverent. The unschooled apostles were haranguing village-corner rustics, and through their amateurism one could sense their sincerity, their uncertainty—and their instants of inspiration.

No bread, no scrip, no money in our purse—

When they came to the end of the reprise, a chord was plucked from a guitar. An arpeggio modulated into a minor key—and another voice filled the auditorium.

Be shod with sandals—

Wayne Larner—

At first there was what seemed to be horror on and around the stage. Kenworthy noticed that the sound technician, who had been leaning back in cynically affected boredom throughout the scene, now leaped to his control console.

'No, no, leave it!' the producer shouted. 'This could be the answer.'

Silence, now, and attention was mesmerized. Kenworthy had never been a Larner fan. He had heard him in his time—who hadn't?—but had never considered him worth listening to. Now he wondered if he had been missing something. This was a superb recording of a superb performance: the overtones, the undertones, the delusion of sincerity. Perhaps it had not even been a delusion.

After the last chord, the sound engineer switched off his reels with an exaggeratedly casual gesture. Simon called Peter forward to speak the curtain line. And Hajek leaped to his feet.

'All right! Cut! Twenty minutes for coffee and nicotine.'

Furnival went over to speak to the producer, and beckoned Kenworthy to come with him.

'How's this for a Godsend? Isn't a disembodied Christ the answer that's been eluding us since square one? Larner's voice—*et praeterea nihil*?'

He went up to the man at the sound console.

'How much of Larner have you got on tape, Lindop?'

'Pretty well the lot. Though it's not all up to that quality.'

'But it will edit?'

'We'll try.'

Furnival's laughter had a light touch of falsetto hysteria.

'This might even make Dyer happy. I dare say there are terms he would accept.'

A different sound rose as they were leaving the theatre. Not all the play took place on the plane that they had just witnessed. Hajek had moved them back to the *Prologue in Chaos*. It was not a taste in orchestration that Kenworthy was ever likely to acquire.

CHAPTER 8

Furnival and Kenworthy had met somewhere during the war, and then after it at some convention or other, while Kenworthy was still at the Yard. Early on the Sunday morning, Furnival had telephoned Kenworthy. Would he come up here (at a fee at which Kenworthy's mind boggled) and keep his eye on things in a quiet way? His specific brief was to watch the interests of the production. He was not going to be expected to compete with the Derbyshire police. What Furnival really wanted, Kenworthy decided, was to have someone on hand who could interpret what the police were up to at any given moment.

Kenworthy had been happy to oblige. The fee meant a family continental holiday next year, and he had had two fascinating if abrasive brushes with Derbyshire in his inspectorial days: once on a case in which he had actually worked with Gleed. He and Gleed had liked each other, once preliminary hazards had sorted themselves out. They might even have remained friends, if either of them had had time to keep contacts alive.

Before he had been on the production site long, there was uncharitable criticism of Kenworthy. Onlookers saw nothing to persuade them that he was moving himself. He wandered about the theatre and its adjoining lots, smiling at those he met—the sort of smile one might see on the face of someone convalescing from an enfeebling illness. Now and then he asked a question, but it was always a trivial one, and if the answer was evasive, he did not press his point. He went on his way with another kind of smile—a sort of apology for having been importunate.

He made several attempts to see Gleed, the first within minutes of his arrival, but Gleed was always somewhere else.

His headquarters staff were courteous but unforthcoming. It was not clear whether this was the way Gleed had briefed them, or whether they spontaneously resented a retired professional coming on the scene on the side of private enterprise.

Gleed was constantly adding to his extensive tactical HQ. He had a report centre in one of the contractors' huts on the theatre site that Lord Furnival had put at his disposal. And equipment—filing cabinets, telephone handsets, trestle tables and folding chairs—kept arriving in great strength. Even the man-power servicing this complex was extravagant. It must be making great demands on the Force's overtime, if not undermining their efficiency in other vital areas.

One of the first calls that Kenworthy made was on the Culvers. He found Joan looking ill and fatigued, her mind seemingly sluggish at first. She did not want to answer questions.

'Have I got to go into it all again? There's nothing I could possibly add to what I told Mr Gleed, and he made me go into it three or four times. And I'd already told Mr Fewter all I could.'

'There is a difference,' Kenworthy said. 'I am a man without standing. I have no authority, no sanctions up my sleeve. If you don't want to talk to me, I shan't try to force you to. I know what you must be feeling.'

At that moment, her father came into the room, a man with the old-fashioned working man's habit of social courtesy.

'Mr Kenworthy—you won't remember me—'

Spontaneous pleasure to see him—but Kenworthy had no memory of having met him before.

'You wouldn't—no—but we did exchange a few words when you were here the last time.'

It was years ago that Kenworthy had been in this area: the murder of a young woman probation officer. He had talked to many men and women. What was routine to a detective-inspector might be a memorable event to people who only had dealings with the CID once in their lives.

'I came for a word with your daughter, but she isn't feeling up to it.'

The old man looked at Joan as if she disappointed him.

'But you'll let us offer you something? Tea—coffee?'

'Coffee would just fill the bill.'

Old Culver started for the kitchen, but Joan said she would make it, obviously relieved to escape from the room. When she came back, Kenworthy noticed that she had not brought a mug for herself. It was only a trivial thing, but it looked as if she felt under the need to withdraw from all things.

'If there's anything you could tell Mr Kenworthy, it would be wrong of you not to help him,' her father said.

She shrugged it off.

'You've heard me speak of him, haven't you? How many years ago is it now? Fifteen?'

In how many other families had Kenworthy's casual questions become a legend? Joan smiled meagrely.

'Oh yes. I've heard the story. More than once.'

'Perhaps I'd better apologize for that,' Kenworthy said.

'Oh, take no notice of me. Life isn't normal.'

'Of course it's not.'

'If only last week hadn't happened.'

'If only they'd set up their damned theatre in North Wales, or on Salisbury Plain,' old Culver said.

'No—don't say that, Father. It could have been a wonderful play.'

'It still may be,' Kenworthy said.

She looked surprised at his optimism.

And, one way or another, without compulsion, she did tell her story—without at first seeming conscious that she was launching out on it. She told about the taxi to Buxton, about shopping in the rain, about the brief visit to the hotel

—this part loosely skipped. Kenworthy noticed a change in her tone, in her speed of speech. At that stage she was making herself unnaturally casual. But he did not take her up on it.

'I'm not going to plague you with a lot more questions, Miss Culver.'

'Thank God for that. Mr Gleed behaved as if he thought I was involved in it somehow—as if I was in some sort of conspiracy.'

'That was Gleed doing his job. A policeman has to play with every possibility.'

'I suppose there have to be policemen. I'm sorry, Mr Kenworthy—I shouldn't have said that.'

'There's another thing I must ask, and you possibly don't know the answer: Who knew that Larner had retrieved his car from the garage in Buxton?'

'How do you mean—who knew?'

'I mean were you, as far as you know, seen by anyone who knew you, either at the garage or on the road? This is a very important question, Miss Culver, because whoever strewed those spikes on the road above Brackdale must have known that Larner was driving. That's assuming that the spikes were meant for him, and let's assume that, for the sake of thinking things through.'

'Well, Wayne's so-called bodyguard knew. They followed us from Buxton to Macclesfield.'

She was clearly striving hard to remember.

'And then there was a funny little man I've seen about the village and the theatre. A man in a dark suit, always carrying a musical instrument about with him.'

'Where did he see you?'

'He was on the pavement outside the garage as we came out.'

'Interesting.'

She frowned. She seemed completely to have overcome her reluctance to talk, and was thinking fast.

'But it couldn't have been any of them, could it? Somebody must have known *when* Wayne was going to drive up the hill. If the spikes had been put there much earlier than they were, there'd have been a pile-up of cars.'

'How right you are, Miss Culver! So it must have been someone at the nightclub, you think?'

'I don't know who. There were people from the *Passion* there, but I don't know them all. The room was so full, and you know what the lighting is like in these places. There were, of course, The Deviants—they are one of the lesser groups in the show, and were also giving a turn at The Grey Cat that night. And Jimmy Lindop, the sound engineer from the show—he was there looking after their amplifiers. But it can't have been any of them, can it?'

'Why not?'

'Because their turn came on very late—after Wayne's, after Wayne and I had gone. They didn't arrive until we were nearly ready to leave. So they couldn't have had anything to do with spikes up Brackdale Hill, could they?'

'They couldn't have put them there,' Kenworthy said, 'but there is such a thing as the telephone, even in the High Peak of Derbyshire. This may all be a waste of time, though. He may have decided in advance that he was going to get his car out. He might have told somebody or other back here.'

'I don't think so, Mr Kenworthy. It was a sudden idea. I can picture even now how it came to him. And I was responsible—for persuading him, I mean—for pushing him over the brink. It seemed outrageous, treating a grown man, an *important* man, like a schoolboy on probation. And he was a splendid driver.'

'I'm sure he was.'

'Oh, but if only I hadn't made Freddy Kershaw try to get my bag back!'

'*Made* him, Miss Culver?'

'That's what it amounted to—it's no use pretending. I

did want it back, and though I didn't say so in so many
words, he knew that. He wanted to do anything he could to
please me.'

CHAPTER 9

Kenworthy ran into Nall and Fewter when he walked up
the hill to take a look for himself at the spot where the car
had run into the wall. Nall was there, looking closely at the
contour and camber of the road. And that in itself seemed
a little odd, since Gleed would surely have had the place
examined and important measurements taken by traffic
specialists as a very early priority.

Today's weather, in the fickle way of early spring, was
ideal for savouring landscape. Sunlight was beginning to
warm swelling tree-buds and a bank undulated with celan-
dines.

Nall did not spot Kenworthy immediately, so Kenworthy
stood and watched him. He was interested to know what
the nature of the sergeant's interest was, and to get into
affable conversation with him if possible. But Nall saw him
at the critical second—and did not know him by sight.

'Just a moment—Press, are you? Identity?'

'I have none,' Kenworthy said pleasantly. 'At least, not
in the sense that identity sometimes carries clout. Simon
Kenworthy, private individual—'

'So what interests you up here, Mr Kenworthy?'

'I'm just enjoying the rugged landscape, sniffing the air,
and revelling in the approach of spring.'

'Well, there's good air and good landscape over many a
square mile of this county. I find sightseers off-putting when
I've work to do. And we've no need for private investigators
on this patch.'

'There are two ways of pointing a thing like that out,

Sergeant—and yours is the one I don't like,' Kenworthy
said, but he said it so mildly that Nall was slow to rise to
the provocation. The encounter had, however, been heard
by Detective-Inspector Fewter, who had just come in sight
from higher up the road.

'Is this man giving you trouble, Sergeant?'

'Not that you'd notice. His name's Kenworthy.'

'Ah yes—I heard you'd arrived, Kenworthy. On Lord
Furnival's payroll now, I believe. Well, don't get in our
way, will you? We don't care for meddlers.'

'I shouldn't think you'll get many,' Kenworthy said agreeably. 'Or that much ready assistance is forthcoming, either.'

'What is that supposed to mean?'

'Forthcoming? I was using it in the sense of ready, willing.
And assistance means help, information, cooperation. In
my experience, both best lubricated by patience and good
manners. Not by the style you adopt. What are you looking
for, by the way? Something that Traffic found and you
missed?'

'Clever bugger,' Fewter said loudly to Nall as Kenworthy
moved away.

Kenworthy went over to the Hall to talk to Cantrell. Cantrell
was clearly another who regarded him as a usurper. But it
was also clear that Cantrell was having to play things
carefully with Furnival at the moment, and dared not be
too abrasive. Instead, he pretended a languorous boredom
with the whole affair. He also made himself out to be
overwhelmed with work.

'Happy to tell you anything you want to know. Gladly
show you round the place—all my alarums and gadgets—
but not just now, if you'll forgive me. Supposed to be in four
other places at this moment. His Lordship is a little on the
testy side since he lost his leading lout.'

'Don't let me hold you up. There were just one or two
little questions.'

'Honestly, Kenworthy, I haven't much time.'

'Won't take a second. How soon last Saturday did you learn that Larner had liberated his car?'

'Within three minutes of its happening. One of his body-guards stayed behind in Buxton to phone me. The whole bloody crew might as well have done, for all they achieved in Macclesfield.'

'And what was your reaction?'

'Absolute joy, old man. Ready to welcome anything that might persuade his Lordship to get rid of Larner.'

'At least you're honest. Don't you think that that might be a dangerous admission? You do see, don't you, Cantrell, how important it is for us to know how many people were aware that Larner was back at the wheel—and would be driving himself home that night?'

Cantrell's face had become unexpectedly suffused with blood.

'Not accusing me of anything, are you, Kenworthy?'

Kenworthy smiled at him, provocatively amiable.

'May I ask two other questions, please? Do you speak Urdu?'

'*Urdu?*'

It was a favourite device of Kenworthy's—asking in all apparent seriousness a question that had no visible purpose. It could worry men of a certain mentality.

'Urdu? No, Kenworthy—my time was after the Raj.'

'Yes, of course. Stupid of me. Were you ever in Northern Ireland?'

'No, I'd finished my time before the present troubles started. But I don't see—'

'Never mind. I was on the wrong track. Thinking of quite a different chap. Just one more. Would you mind telling me who the two men were that you ejected from the theatre this morning?'

'Oh, them! Young Harpur, hobbledehoy, lout, needs a good hiding, conceited, work-shy young oaf. Best brain in the county at the age of seven, according to fond parents. Goes about nowadays looking like a drooling imbecile. If you ask my opinion, that's one of his brain's built-in defences against the dreaded word *work*.'

'And the other chap?'

'Equally barmy—only in a different direction. Alfie Tandy. Got bees in his bonnet about every damned thing under the sun.'

'What's his connection with this place?'

'Works for The Deviants—one of the loudest and least harmonious of our groups. Calls himself their road manager. Road manager my arse! Man couldn't manage a game of Bingo. And what would they want with a road manager on a static site like this? The man's a half-wit, helps them load their van when they go out moonlighting. And that's another thing that they've got to account for, these damned Deviants: singing protected songs from the show at pubs in Edale and Doncaster. With any luck we might be saying goodbye to The Deviants too.'

'Have you ever been to Doncaster?' Kenworthy asked him.

'Doncaster? Doncaster—oh, it must have been all of twenty years ago. A race meeting when I was stationed at Catterick.'

'Thanks a lot,' Kenworthy said, 'I'll be off now. Mustn't interfere with your work.'

CHAPTER 10

Kenworthy knocked on Dyer's door. Dyer asked him to sit down, his dark eyes burning with unreadable concerns.

Some men fancied that they understood Dyer's basic motivations. A standard range of stories went the rounds about him. Kenworthy had dropped on information—of a kind—about Dyer before he had set out for Derbyshire. A few years ago, one of the Sunday Supplements had done a thing about Dyer. To assess it, you had to remember what public it was written for. Kenworthy remembered it vaguely, and was certain that it would be one of the things that his daughter had never cleared out of her bedroom cupboard when she left home to get married. And it was still there— on top of a pile of her discarded LPs: Buddy Holly and Little Richard. Because at the age when Joan Culver was being fed the knowledge of the pop scene that the likes of Dyer wanted her to have, so was Karen Kenworthy.

Dyer had fads. They were not luxuries. You might call them eccentric attachments. Deprived of them, people said, he was inclined to sulk. There was a certain type of denture-cleaner, for example, not even a brand of spectacular repute or efficiency, that he bought wholesale and carried about with him in absurd quantity. He was fussy about his toilet paper, of which he took a dozen or more rolls with him on any journey. It was coarse-textured stuff. He would use only one kind of synthetic sweetener in his coffee, and was apt to become restive if he had less than a fortnight's supply in reserve. Also he suffered chronically from insomnia. If he had a conscience, the writer had amended the Wodehouse quote, he might conceivably have something on it.

Dyer had come out of the army at the end of the Second World War with rather more behind him than the gratuity due to an RASC Captain. The Sunday journalists did not go so far as to suggest that he had fiddled along the lines of communication in France and Belgium, but they reported how he had once been held up and minutely searched by Customs on his way home on leave. Nothing was found on him. Clearly he got a kick out of living on his wits. His first civilian living had been eked out on the legitimate edge of the army surplus trade. But he had never been one of the big operators. His profits did not resemble theirs, and when there were arrests in the late 1940s, he was not caught in the trawl. Dyer had always been remarkable for stopping short of major legal risks. He knew his law, had a photographic memory for small print clauses, and the older he got, the more rigorously did he stay on the right side of them.

It was not until the mid-'fifties, on the crest of Rock'n'Roll, that he began to dabble in popular entertainment. He bought a partnership to revive a flagging agency—not Charing Cross Road stuff, simply moving semi-amateur skiffle groups about in places like Deptford and New Cross. The public he was catering for were the sort who talked of going *tooled-up* to their revels—with coshes, loaded belts, even choppers under their jackets. But Dyer had nothing to do with this imitative gang warfare. In the early days he was not even much concerned with musical talent. In the heyday of the washboard and the tea-chest bass, he scouted for groups, recruited and rostered them, saw that they turned up where they were booked, and were minimally equipped to satisfy their fans. They had to be youngsters with enough stamina to stand up to the squalor and the hours. Most of them were not gifted enough to have earned regular money through any agency but Dyer's.

That was at first. He soon became sickened by mediocrity. By now he knew a good deal about what the pop public wanted. He worked on the means of spreading fashions and fulfilling the demand for them. There had to be traces of individualism, but it had to be an individualism that could be ruthlessly governed. He scouted round for marketable, trainable, governable talent. And he found Wayne Larner.

When Dyer first billed The Stalagmites, it was by the name under which he had first found them performing. Their material and their execution were equally lamentable. So were their personalities, except for their lead singer. But Dyer did not interfere with them immediately. He let them continue together for a fortnight. Then he sacked all but Larner, paying the others a flat week's money. He paid the going rate to get Larner an audition: more than one recording company at this time was looking for a new name to bait its hooks with. The adolescent market thought it knew what it wanted. It did not know how effectively its wants were being moulded. Larner was malleable. Many people had tried to guess how much Dyer spent on plugging Larner's early titles. He found him the song that was his first rave success: *Forty Shades of Blue*. It paid for Larner's first honeymoon—with Sue Bistort, who had graced the school register under the name of Bickerstaffe. Dyer used his share of the proceeds to buy a substantial holding in a pirate radio ship, the plugging machine *par excellence*, but he pulled out when a Westminster lobby began to get restive—his nervous eye always on legality. But by then he had the supply and demand for Wayne Larner beautifully balanced. *Blue Baby* sold a million. Larner went twice to the States, came back with his Filipino, ditched Sue Bistort. Dyer added new names to his stable: Sally Foster-Lunn, The Whodunnits. Names rose and fell in the charts. Larner's stayed steady.

Dyer could have lived opulently. By now he had a headquarters cadre: lyricists and composers whom he paid enough—and who had large enough collections of rejection slips—not to care who got the credit as long as they got the cash. Starlets had to be drilled in speech and posture—in some cases, even in table manners. Some jibbed at the discipline—and found themselves derelict. Styles changed, but Dyer kept Larner in the top league. His ghost-written autobiography was well up in another breed of chart.

What interested Dyer was making money, not making use of it. He lived less stridently than many a suburban executive. He had a reasonable house at Pangbourne, but it was modest by the standards of his neighbours. He drank no more than an occasional bottle of light ale. He did not like spirits, was happy with supermarket wines, did not smoke. He ran an old Cortina and was married to a self-effacing wife, by whom he had two girls and a boy who went to a very minor public school. He had no sexual adventures. He was no spender, but it wasn't for the hoarding of it that he liked money. It was for the getting of it. He was said to be a bastard to negotiate with.

Dyer was glad to see Kenworthy. He badly wanted to talk. He was looking moodily out of his window when he called to Kenworthy to come in. The superstructure of the proscenium arch was just visible over the tree-tops. It was a frank imitation of Oberammergau, with the back of the stage open to a living backcloth of green hills.

'Let's hope that now you've come, we're going to see some sense. Anyone would think I was Gleed's number one suspect, the way he asked me what I was doing on Saturday night. Christ—if ever a man had anything to lose! And I wish that silly bastard Furnival would let his mind stay made up. Look how he's dithered about these Mary Magdalenes. I could have given him the choice of half a dozen at overnight notice, ranging from coloratura to Gospel Rock. Do you know what he suggested to me at breakfast this morning? To have Christ played by a woman. The name of Bridget Doyle has been mentioned, do you mind! How would that be for gimmickry? He says that on Shakespeare's stage, the lead was always played by a girl. Says it would go down big with the feminists.'

'I should have thought you'd known him long enough,' Kenworthy said, 'to know when he's pulling your leg.'

'In any case, it wouldn't surprise me if Larner turns up again yet. He's capable of having gone to ground for a bit. I wouldn't put it past him to have taken himself off to London for a few days.'

'If he's still alive.'

'He must have been alive to have got out of that car, mustn't he? Don't any of you know what I've lost, if Larner's dead? Does anybody know what I put into Larner—and I don't mean money? I doubt whether Larner had ever heard of the New Testament before we showed him this script. He thought *Christ* was something you said when your shoelace broke. Can you picture him, the night I found him, Kenworthy? It was in a cellar in Finsbury Park, the Stalag, a one-room nightclub, seating about twenty-five, average age not a day more than seventeen. There were seventy in there, and they stank. It was done up to look like a prisoner-of-war hutment, because that was the décor Izzy Ginsberg found there when he took on the lease. The Stalagmites. Four quid a night between them, so that Izzy could sell instant coffee at five bob a cup. Three yobbos and one girl. Verminous, the place was. I bought a stone of DDT and dusted myself from head to foot, the only night I sat through the floor show at the Stalag.'

Dyer's talk kept his anger on the boil.

'Their idea of the big time was cans of crap from the Delicatessen. Fish, chips and paw-paws. And it looked as if they were taking it in turns with Susan Bistort, as they called her. Bickerstaffe, her name was—Larner's first marriage. Later, when I was beginning to get him four figures for an engagement, she had both her eyes blacked when a gang of adolescents mobbed them at Heathrow. They set up home in Virginia Water—and then I wouldn't let her go to America with him. Damn it, man, she was five months pregnant. What would that have done to the image? Larner came back with his South Sea Island piece. "All I want," Susan told the columnists, "is for Wayne to be happy." Do you know what it cost me to get that said, heard and printed?'

'It beats me how you spot these people,' Kenworthy said. 'Would you reckon to groom practically anyone you picked? If so, you can have a go at me if you like. Singing ex-fuzz: mightn't that go down big?'

But that strain of humour was alien to Dyer's mood. He went off tangentially.

'I know what you're thinking, and you're wrong, Kenworthy. Larner had what it takes. He had all that it takes, and a bonus. His body, his limbs, his hair, his skin—after I'd persuaded him to wash it and keep it washed. Perhaps you never got near enough to him to notice the texture of his skin? He had a voice, too—once we'd taught him not to try too hard. God, when I listen to some of those early recordings, even now, I could bloody well weep. We even managed to teach him to play more than the three regulation chords on his guitar. There was a number he sang for the first time in this theatre last week: *Trodden Palms*. It had stage-hands dabbing their eyes with their cuffs.'

'Yes. I can see what you stand to lose, Dyer. But it isn't the first time you've lost him, is it? Ten years you had to get by without him, didn't you?'

Dyer spread his hands.

'His contract came up for renewal, and he wouldn't sign on reasonable terms, wanted a glutton's share of the takings. He thought that it was *his* ability that had got him where he was, that always was his trouble. And there were plenty of so-called agents waiting round the corner for him with promises.'

'Is any of what you're saying true in any respect, Dyer?'

Dyer looked at him wildly.

'What do you mean by that?'

'I mean you might as well tell the truth to me, who has neither rank nor office, than wait for it to be dug out by Gleed and Fewter and Co. Because they're going to find it, Dyer. There are going to be some pretty sharp-edged inquiries. It isn't through neglect that Gleed's spending a lot of his time out of Peak Low. He knows where the answer might lie. There's been more than one round of bother in your log-book of Larner, hasn't there? Didn't something rather special happen in Nottingham?'

'Why does that have to keep rearing its head?'

'Because such things have that habit. Tell me what happened.'

Dyer was quick-witted enough to know that what

Kenworthy said made sense.

'He seduced a girl who spent her living days in a wheel-chair. Ex polio. Paraplegic. He laid her. Myself, I always believed that she wasn't uncooperative—to the best of her ability. But her father sussed it out and played all kinds of hell, saw what he was on to. She was too scared to tell the truth.'

'You mean the truth as you'd like to see it. And you bought them off?'

'I paid compensation,' Dyer said, with self-convincing piety. 'And made bloody sure that Larner contributed the lion's share.'

'Using the hoary old stand-by, I suppose, of saving her from the witness-box. So Larner was that sort of bastard, was he?'

'You didn't know him, Kenworthy. He could have had the pick of three or four thousand prize tarts in any town he sang in. And he did. But he liked now and then to get hold of some girl so damned unendowed, for preference deformed, that he got the feeling that he really meant something to her. That was the way his mind worked. He liked being that kind of Prince Charming. But once was enough for him with most of his Sleeping Beauties. Kenworthy, when you've had all there is to be had a thousand times over by the time you're nineteen, you go looking in strange places for new angles.'

'So he didn't branch out, Dyer. You dropped him. And now you've brought him back. And you find he's learned nothing. Nothing's changed. Rehearsals have barely started, and he's having it away with Ricarda Mommsen. Tell me this about Larner, Dyer—did he turn his back on everybody who had to do with the old days—The Stalagmites?'

'Is it Alfie Tandy and Jimmy Lindop you're thinking of? They should never have let anybody from the Stalag era on to this campus. Have you come across Alfie Tandy yet—a silly bugger who goes about with all his gear in a broken-

down old banjo-case? Alfie was the uncle of one of the kids
in the original group. The mother was widowed and had
swanned off God knows where. The kid was grandmother-
reared, and this nut-case uncle was the only male influence
in his life. Well, I'll give Alf Tandy his due. He was as
clueless about the pop scene as he was about growing boys
—but he did back those youngsters. He'd no idea of music,
outside a knees-up, but if the lads were friends of his
nephew's, then they must be good. He found them an old
warehouse to practise in. He paid the hire purchase deposit
on cheap instruments. He got them dates with Izzy Ginsberg
—and saw to it that Izzy paid up. And, of course, he took
it amiss when I wanted Larner. I broke the group up. How
much longer could they have lasted? And where would
Larner have got with them round his neck?'

'You mentioned another name just now. Lindop, was it?'

'Jimmy Lindop. He was the only Stalagmite with a modi-
cum of brains. He looked after their electronics. The sort of
kid you'd never see without a screwdriver or a soldering
iron in his hand. He attended to their mikes and amplifiers.
It's a wonder they weren't all electrocuted more than once.
He didn't know much—but he never stopped learning.
When The Stalagmites broke up, he went to Technical
College, got down to it properly. I won't deny that he's now
one of the best acoustic engineers in the business. But I'd
never have given him a job on the same production as
Wayne Larner. I told Furnival and Cantrell so—but they
preferred not to listen. At least, Furnival made an idiotic
joke about it and Colonel Sir Echo can be relied on to laugh
on cue.'

'And what's Lindop's status here?'

'Chief Sound Engineer. And I've dropped all the hints I
could the way of Gleed. He ought to be asking Jimmy
Lindop what he was doing on Saturday night.'

'Purely as a matter of interest,' Kenworthy said, 'what
did you tell Gleed you were doing on Saturday night?'

'No alibi at all,' Dyer told him. 'As far as time and place
were concerned, I made myself available for any crime that
Gleed cared to nail on me. I spent the evening in my own
room, had no visitors and no phone calls—just drank two
glasses of white wine over a John le Carré. I won't say
Gleed looked happy about it, but he didn't hammer at it
over-much.'

'Because there was nothing for him to hammer at. When
I was in the Force I eventually came to the conclusion that
no alibi was sometimes Bill Sykes's safest bet, if he really
wanted to impress.'

CHAPTER 11

Every day in some little way the stage-set looked as if
an eventual public performance might be feasible. Newly
painted canvas flats would appear, the shepherds' cauldron,
the pillars of the Temple. And sometimes these things would
vanish again to have fresh things done to them—as was the
case of the Sepulchre, which was scheduled to be brought
back into the action on the morning of Kenworthy's second
day in Peak Low. But it was not brought back; because
when the scene-shifters went to fetch it from its dock, they
found a body in it—a murderer's final act of cynicism—of
blasphemy, some said.

But this news was slow to reach Kenworthy, who at the
time was taking a leisurely walk planned to bring him past
a twentieth-century house at the lower end of the village,
where a brook made its way down a broad valley to a deeper
cleft. Since the heart of Peak Low was protected by the
planners, it was only on this southern outer ring that any new
building was allowed. But Notre Abri had been sensitively
co-ordinated with the rest of the settlement, and a few years'
weathering of its locally quarried stone would enable it to

hold up its head among neighbours two centuries its senior.

No one would have thought that the house interested him, but Kenworthy took note of Laura Ashley curtains, bookcases covering whole areas of wall, and a large abstract painting in pastel shades: a home in which funds and educated taste were not lacking. He sauntered past and returned at a gentle pace through a field that brought him close to the rear of the property, separated from the back garden only by a low drystone wall. There were several sheds, all in good trim, and two of them served by mains electricity, borne from the house on heavy duty cable. A youth was carrying into one of these sheds a half-finished wooden model of a boat, powered by a spirit motor. He had roughly cut, longish hair, whose styling obviously did not interest him. The last time Kenworthy had seen him, Cantrell was ejecting him from the theatre. Kenworthy tried to catch his eye, but it was an eye that did not care for human contact.

'Looks a nice little job you've got there,' Kenworthy said. Young Harpur grunted something unintelligible and vanished into the shed. Kenworthy climbed the wall—which would have been an ill-advised action by a serving policeman—crossed to the shed and looked in at the door. He saw an interesting collection of unidentified equipment. The shelves were filled to capacity, everything neatly labelled with Dymo tape. Most of the objects seemed to be working models of considerable complexity: some belt-driven, some cog-driven, some cam-controlled. There were a lathe and a power drill. The youth looked up as Kenworthy entered: he was planing a flank of his craft.

'Some original ideas you have here.'

The lad grunted again. Kenworthy did not propose to show anything but friendship.

'What's this one?'

He was looking at a water-pump with a heavy flywheel, apparently water-powered by gravity-feed. Harpur took his time before he looked round again, and when he did he seemed to be considering whether to answer or not. But he did answer.

'Kid's stuff. Used to play about with perpetual motion.'

Contemptuous—even, it seemed, of his past self. His voice was grating, as if it had only recently broken—which could hardly have been the case.

'Had ideas about that myself, when I was a boy,' Kenworthy said brightly, 'though I never got round to making a prototype: I fancied a dynamo that drove a motor that powered the dynamo.'

'Wouldn't work,' the youth said. 'Too much energy loss from engine-friction. No way round that.'

'That's what my physics teacher told me, when I was at school,' Kenworthy said, with heavy parody of ruefulness, but the lad was apparently not given to humour.

'What's that you're working on now, then?'

'Submarine.'

He turned his back on Kenworthy and went on with his planing. Kenworthy waited until he paused to test the balance of his model across the palm of his hand.

'Where do you mean to sail her, then?'

'Water-swallow. Up in Meeting House Dale. Want to chart it, but it's too narrow to crawl in.'

'Won't you risk losing her?'

'Radio control.'

He bent back to his work. Kenworthy looked about himself, taking in greater detail. And he saw at the back of a bench a couple of Z-shaped spikes that were surely of the type that had been used up Brackdale Hill. There were vices and blacksmith's tongs and even a small forge in a corner: certainly enough equipment to have made the infernal things here.

Kenworthy stretched across and picked them up. Harpur saw the action, and his attitude changed immediately. Kenworthy could see that his hands were shaking.

'Where did you get these—and what do you use them for?'

He kept his voice gentle and his tone was as factual. But that was insufficient to put Julian Harpur back at his ease. He seemed to be having difficulty in accommodating his Adam's apple.

'Did you make them yourself?'

The lad could only produce the sort of sound that might come from a deaf mute. But at least he was trying to get something out.

'I found them here.'

'Here?'

'Somebody put them here.'

Kenworthy made a quick decision. He was not going on with this. He knew that he could handle this boy as well as anyone could, but that was not the point. He had to be handled by the man who was going to carry the whole action through—and that man was Gleed. There were telephone wires to the cottage and he would ring Gleed from here, stay here making innocent conversation, get Julian Harpur back on to the subject of his models until Gleed or one of his officers arrived.

But it was not so simple.

'Who are you? What are you doing here? What's going on?'

The voice was a woman's from the doorway—no doubt the boy's mother—a woman a few years into her forties in a denim skirt with a Tenerife sweat-shirt, and one of those hairstyles that look like a haphazard tangle but are presumably consciously planned and cost money.

'My name's Kenworthy.'

'That isn't a passport to anywhere—least of all to private premises.'

Kenworthy had heard the Harpurs' name several times in his short stay here, and everyone who had spoken it had laid the blame for the youth's condition squarely on his mother's stupidity. The father commuted to Derby, where he was a design engineer. He spent more time out of Peak

Low than in it and his wife set the tone of their domestic life. She hadn't a friend in the village, though she had by now been here twenty years. She was an intellectual snob —as well as a snob in other areas that it was difficult to define—and had brought up their son in the confident belief that he had talents out of the ordinary and was a soul apart from these hill-folk.

'I came in to speak to this young man. We were talking about the model he is making—and about perpetual motion in general.'

She saw then the spikes that he was still holding.

'And to plant those things here, I suppose. I can quite understand that the police greatly prefer to have that sort of chore done for them by men without official standing. Julian—go into the house.'

He obeyed with resentment, but as if he had no will of his own.

'I suppose you think Julian's fair game,' she said.

Relaxed, she might have been an attractive woman, but Kenworthy wondered if she ever were relaxed. There were forty-odd years of confident superiority here, but that, ingrained though it was, must surely by now hide a complex turbulence. Had she completely failed to come to terms with the fact that her beliefs had got her nowhere? Must it be everyone else who was wrong?

'I would like to use your telephone, please.'

'Certainly not. I do not propose to be a party to adducing false evidence. Kindly hand those things to me. Since you claim to have found them here, they are my property.'

'You know what they are, do you?'

'I can guess. I am capable of reading newspaper reports.'

'So how do you account for their being here—ignoring your childish suggestion that I brought them?'

'Don't waste my time, Mr Kenworthy. Put the things down and go.'

Her attitude must cloak some measure of uncertainty.

She dared not risk leaving him to go into the house. He, on the other hand, knew that if he parted with the spikes and left, they would disappear without trace. It was a pity that a woman as wrong-headed as Mrs Harpur believed so fervently in the stance that she was taking.

There was no tidy way of extricating himself from the situation. He sized up the lie of the workshop. It would mean barging past her through the door, possibly having to shoulder her aside. He was not sure whether she would actually attack him. He would have to dash across the yard, could easily vault the wall, would then have the freedom of the field.

He moved his shoulders as if he were going back to the work-bench. She took a step forward to try to stop him— and he was past her and out of the door. Only when he pulled himself up breathless in the field did he wonder why he was still running.

He rang the Incident HQ to report his find, was told that Gleed was away for the rest of the day. A Chief Inspector, whom he did not know, was temporarily in charge. He took the Z-irons from him and promised that Gleed would be in touch.

The country was told in the news bulletins that night that an unnamed man was helping inquiries. Peak Low bristled with the unsurprising tale that it was Julian Harpur who had been driven over to Derby.

A formal press release let it be known that Larner had died from roughly inflicted injuries to his head, and that it was not yet determined whether these had been incurred in the car crash.

CHAPTER 12

Freddy Kershaw had taken to buying several daily papers and it always looked as if they had pages of situations vacant. But practically every job demanded some skill or semi-skill that he did not possess. It was an infamously bad time to be looking for employment. Not that his mind was fully made up. It still depended, he told himself, on how they treated him when he was up before the Board next week. Was he still in any doubt about the outcome?

Personnel Management—A few years' experience necessary— Degree in sociology—The successful candidate will have worked for some years—

His landlady struggled up to tap on the door of his bed-sit. She had always assured him that the stairs did not worry her, but her attitude to him had cooled since this had blown up.

'A gentleman downstairs for you.'

'Did he give his name?'

'I'd say he was an official gentleman.'

A Derbyshire woman, a country woman come to town, she'd have thought it bad manners to ask an official gentle-man his name. She was obliging and motherly, but not all of her had arrived in this century yet.

'I'll come down.'

'You can take him into the sitting-room,' she said, but he knew she was hoping he wouldn't. She was watching *Crossroads*.

'No. I'll bring him up here.'

At the door was a neatly dressed, dignified man, no longer young.

'My name's Kenworthy.'

Kershaw had a sharp memory and knew many Yard

names. In the years when he had lived for detection, he had
read all the casework he could lay his hands on. His taste
for all that had finished a week ago.

'Got somewhere we can natter?'

'A bit untidy, sir. I dare say I can clear somewhere for
you to sit.'

Shirts, socks, underwear, books higgledy-piggledy. Kershaw had not been expecting visitors.

'Made a pig's ear of it, didn't you?' Kenworthy asked.

Kershaw bristled. So Kenworthy took the same view as
the rest of them. For a moment he was tempted to answer
tactlessly—or not at all. What did Kenworthy want here?
Kershaw began to understand why a child sometimes sulks:
it is the last feeble hope of making opposition go away.

'I know how you feel,' Kenworthy said. 'I've not been in
your precise spot, but I've had spots of my own in my time.'

He wasn't smiling, but he had none of the pomposity that
Kershaw would have expected of him.

'I've stopped thinking about it. I've said what had to be
said and now all I can do is stick to it and wait.'

'Shit or bust, we used to call it. But then I was brought
up in a vulgar school. *And for God's sake don't make me go over
it again:* is that what you're thinking?'

Kershaw told himself to think before he opened his mouth.
The words readiest to his tongue would have helped no one.

Oh, piss off—

'I don't know that I'd be behaving any differently if I
were in your shoes,' Kenworthy said.

Patronizing sod—

'But you did have three weeks, as I understand it, of
working in and around this circus before the real troubles
started. If my name had been Fewter or Gleed, I'd have
wanted you on the case, whatever else had happened. You
must be a mine of information.'

'Mr Gleed did say that that was what he felt. But by then
things had gone too far for him to do anything about them.'

Kershaw was surprised to hear himself talking affably.

'And, of course, I've given them all the help I could. I've answered all their questions. I've told them everything I know—and some of the things I think.'

'So what do you make of the state of the case now?'

'I know nothing about the state of the case now—and I'm doing my best not to hear anything. I told Gleed all I knew. He told me nothing.'

'You wouldn't expect him to.'

'No.'

'So who had it in for Larner?'

'How can I know that?'

'In your opinion?'

'I don't know enough of the facts to have formed an opinion.'

'Splendid answer. But at least you know who disliked him.'

'A good many people.'

'Not including your lady-friend.'

'She isn't my lady-friend.'

He was in danger of losing his temper again. Possibly Kenworthy wanted that. A man out of control of himself will talk uncircumspectly. They taught you that on the course. And Fewter was always saying it. It was the only item in his methodology.

'No? It's immaterial, anyway. What is more to the point is—are you prepared to help *me*?'

Kenworthy outlined his position vis-à-vis Furnival.

'I'll have to consider it.'

'Well, don't consider it for too long, lad. I'm not asking you to break any laws—or standing orders.'

'You'd better tell me what it is you want me to do.'

'Every time you open your mouth, Kershaw, the better I like your style. Well—first tell me everything that happened in Peak Low last Saturday—*everything*.'

Kershaw did that. And it was only when he reached

the Doncaster match-end that he had found in Ricarda
Mommsen's bed-sit that Kenworthy stirred in his chair.

'Right,' he said. 'Assignment number one—who knew
that Larner was going to drive home from The Grey Cat in
his own car? Do you think you could start working on that?
And just one other thing. That young lady: whether she's
yours or not, she needs company. I wouldn't neglect her too
long.'

A piece of news came down from the hospital. Ricarda had
stirred in her coma and said an audible word, which was
duly noted down by the woman officer on duty beside her
bed.

Wayne—

CHAPTER 13

Kenworthy made a circuit of the grounds, was tempted
towards the theatre by an orchestral burst that reverberated
from the woods. This was wild music, bodisome, rhythmic
and discordant—a cross between *The Hall of the Mountain
King* and *The Entry of the Dahleks*. Szolnok, in an Aran sweater
big enough to envelop three of him, seemed in a mood to
mow down his players with his baton, if only it had been a
sub-machine-gun. On stage, in front of rudimentary scenery,
Larner's understudy, his back to the auditorium, a leather
thong at his wrist, was lashing the money-lenders from the
Temple.

A down-beat chord from Szolnok, a signal to the wings
from Hajek, and a clip of film began to play itself out on a
backstage cyclorama: Threadneedle Street under the silhouette of St Paul's; a bishop's mitre embroidered in cloth
of gold, emeralds glinting in his crozier; a *clochard* in black
rags huddled over a grating within sight of Notre Dame; a

tramp

glass case, glittering with filigrée reliquaries; the marble foyer of a bank, on one of whose leather settees a rotund, tonsured monk was eating a whole roast chicken in his fingers.

In the wings a knot of extras were idling, nibbling at Kit-kat bars, drinking coffee out of plastic tumblers. The sound engineer was sitting at his console, a cigarette on his lower lip, one eye looking up obliquely now and then at the screen, the other keeping track of a heavily annotated script. He seemed adept at dividing his attention, most of which was absorbed in a girlie magazine propped up against his bank of switches. The ultimate spectacle might be lavish, but most of the graft was going on in an atmosphere of bored cynicism.

The Christ figure made a sweeping gesture with his thong. The shadow of the gesture was supposed to cut across the projected image. But the lighting effects were still unperfected, and the result was lame.

'Cut! Cut! Cut!'

Szolnok dropped his stick. The orchestra subsided like mass failing bagpipes. There was an interruption minutes long while electricians experimented with spots and Fresnels. Finally, Hajek decided that this was a problem that had best be solved by technicians on their own—working through the night if need be.

'I want it right before we start tomorrow.'

Szolnok, who had been utterly absorbed in his music, utterly committed to it, sat down with weary resignation. The enmity between him and Hajek had become a legend within weeks. Szolnok, a Pole, came allegedly from aristocratic stock, the young scion of a cavalry family, left over in England by the war. Hajek, the Budapest deviationist, was still at heart a political creature. Only now and then did their hostility break out at rehearsal; more often it expressed itself like this, in silent contempt.

Kenworthy turned to look at the face of the man at the

console: Jimmy Lindop, one-time Stalagmite. He had a smile of faint superiority, nourished by the sight of the show going wrong; a provocatively casual way of attending to his side of the business—and yet an on-the-second efficiency which seemed to cost him no effort. It took more to produce the *Passion* than would be apparent to the Mothers' Union.

'Let's have the last ten seconds of the violence.'

Fast wind of video-tape, then the final expulsion of the usurers. The kaleidoscope translated the exodus into a contemporary environment. The monk, still snatching bites at his chicken, was scurrying into the thick of a city crowd.

From a back seat, Lord Furnival had seen Kenworthy arrive, and now got up to join him.

'All wholesomely radical, I'm sure you will agree.'

'Just as long as your box-office doesn't get itself ejected too.'

'Somehow I don't think the man to do that is likely to honour us with a visit.'

A banker in a morning suit was plunging with a furled umbrella through a group of sightseeing nuns. An oil sheikh was knocked flying on his back. A street-corner preacher was howling assurances of eternal damnation at the backs of the fleeing crowd. He picked up his soap-box and stumbled after them.

Then came peace and calm. The imagery advanced to stained-glass windows: Monet's Rouen, borrowed from *Fantasia*. A requiem was led by the violas and 'cellos, with overtones from a choir of descant clarinets. The understudy struck a pose in silhouette—or in what would be silhouette when the technicians had done their homework. Then came a link-passage, the melody modulated into a new theme on a mightily amplified guitar, intended to be soul-disturbing. Kenworthy decided that it very nearly was. Given the full theatrical illusion, it very well might be—for some. It was a question of over-stimulation—of an audience who would have come, some of them, to have their souls disturbed:

religion on the plane of emotional masturbation. And this was the cue for one of the Larner songs that was due to be manœuvred into multi-million sales.

In the cloisters of my heart—

The *Voice*—with purple light spilling over into gothic aisles.

As in that garden—

A recording: Larner brought *gar-den* up a satisfying fifth. Even the backstage card-players were cocking an ear.

In that cool Syrian shade—

But then something else happened. Larner coughed and stopped singing. The guitar stumbled over a chord, then gave out.

'Sod it! I'm getting pissed off with this. Every time I sing that line, I have to compete with that bloody trombone. Do something about it, Szolnok.'

It was unmistakably Larner's voice. And Hajek spoke, also on the recording:

'Cut! Give him the lead-in again. Cut the trombone altogether, Szolnok.'

Then Hajek spoke in the flesh:

'Scrub it, Lindop!'

Furnival was advancing down the aisle, clambering on to the apron-stage, shouting at the engineer.

'It isn't the first time you've done this to us, Lindop. When are you going to get those tapes sorted out? Don't you have anything properly logged? I don't want this to happen again. Work through the lot—by tomorrow. I want all the false starts taken out and erased.'

'Sorry, sir.'

A cheerful apology. Kenworthy lost himself beyond the fringe of the theatre until the company was dismissed for lunch. Then he stepped unobtrusively into the wings, as Lindop was fast rewinding the last tape he had used.

'Mr Jimmy Lindop, I presume.'

'Correct, sir. And to what do I owe—?'

Mockery: Lindop clearly knew who Kenworthy was. His tone implied that he was prepared to be tolerant of authority, but must not be expected to respect it.

'So what's your next trick, Lindop? Accidentally obliterate every master-tape you've got of Larner? Or play all the duff recordings on the opening night?'

'Now, really, Mr Kenworthy—you shouldn't go about putting ideas into people's heads.'

Kenworthy's tone became as casual as Lindop's.

'It makes a change from harassing one Mary Magdalene after another,' he said.

'Are you accusing me?'

'Not at all. On what grounds could I? Maybe I expressed myself badly. Perhaps I should have said it makes a change from waiting to see what will happen to Mary Magdalene next.'

'I like the sound of that better. It makes me feel less vulnerable.'

'How vulnerable do you feel about the microphone that might have electrocuted Joan Culver?'

'More than vulnerable—resentful. Microphones are strictly my department, and I don't like people buggering about with my toys.'

'And the trapdoor that inexplicably fell open?'

'That's the stage-manager's kingdom. I didn't even know there was a trapdoor there. You really must be careful about the way you sling slander about, Kenworthy. You should think of the consequences. Furnival wouldn't want the shop stewards blowing their whistles, would he?'

'You think you could bring them all out? You think he wouldn't sack the lot of you?'

'Kenworthy—'

'Look: let's come to an understanding, Lindop. Have you thought what sort of a case you might find yourself having to answer? You've dug yourself well into this show. You have possession of Larner's tapes—some superb—and some deplorable. You have unrestricted access to the stage and you have a lot of know-how. I could find plausible motives for you to want Larner to look a fool. So if friend Gleed is being pressed to show interim progress, he might call you in for a prolonged interview. You were the one who used the word vulnerable. How long before Gleed has that microphone down to you?'

'I was the one who jumped up and pulled her away from it.'

'Exactly. Diverting attention away from yourself.'

'Only a bastard would see things that way, Kenworthy.'

'There are bastards about. Some people are going to see things that way. And other things have happened here besides horse-play. A man's dead and a woman's dying. How about somebody trying to stick those coincidences on your ticket too?'

Lindop tried to laugh it off—unconvincingly.

'Could be nasty,' he said. 'Except for one thing. I was fully occupied on Saturday night. In reliable company.'

'I'm glad to hear it. It means you could be in a strong position to help me. I'd like that. So fire away, Lindop. Is there anything you feel you ought to tell me?'

'You're overestimating me. I know very little.'

'You can tell me plenty about the Stalag days—and about Alfie Tandy.'

'That's for sure. I was a foundation non-playing member of The Stalagmites. I could split your sides with the goings-on. But they'd stop short of telling you what happened on Saturday night—because I don't bloody well know. And I'd like to know—for personal reasons.'

'You could tell me what happened in Doncaster.'

'What has Doncaster to do with it?'

'When were you last there?'

'One night early last week. The Deviants were playing away, which isn't exactly flush with their contract. They are a group of triers—not exactly beginners, but they've a long haul to the top—with no Dyer to pull ropes for them. I've been giving them a bit of a hand. They need a few local engagements, because this show has bogged them down. All Furnival has given them is two spots of two and a half minutes each. So anything helps. I rather like them. I like their music, and I like their spirit. That's why I'm safe about Saturday night. They were singing at a club near Edale. I was twiddling the knobs.'

'And the same thing in Doncaster?'

'Doncaster, Barnsley, Rawmarsh, Heckmondwike, Halifax: clubs and pubs. They've been around—all the beauty spots.'

'And Alfie Tandy was in Doncaster too, wasn't he? What was it? A committee meeting, safe from eavesdroppers, of people who had scores to settle with Larner? Was Ricarda Mommsen there too?'

'You've a strong imagination, Kenworthy.'

'Have I? I also once had a reputation for hammering at indicative little facts. Here's something I ought not to divulge, Lindop: did you know that one of Gleed's officers found a Doncaster book-match in Ricarda Mommsen's apartment? That's a characteristic little fact. It *is* a fact—'

'If you say so—'

'And it does give one grounds for thought,' he said. 'So was Ricarda Mommsen at Doncaster?'

'No.'

'You need time to think, don't you, Lindop? Well—you haven't long.' Then he stopped talking because feet were approaching through a backstage door. It was Gleed, and it was Kenworthy he wanted.

They shook hands with unforced heartiness.

CHAPTER 14

Gleed was different from the man Kenworthy remembered. A decade had drawn something over the last of the Derbyshire Detective-Superintendent's youth. What had first struck Kenworthy in their earlier case had been Gleed's boyish appearance for a Chief Inspector. It was a screen from behind which he had loosed off some devastating surprises. Now his hair was not far off white. And although he had never looked lean, he had taken on a modest but perceptible layer of fat. They went for a walk together, away from the theatre, away from the tracks frequented by those connected with the theatre. Kenworthy forwent his lunch, did not mention it. Gleed was at that stage of his career and of this case where meals were not part of the rhythm. He ate when he felt hungry if he happened to have time to spare within reach of food.

'Don't think I don't know—but just what is your brief from Furnival?'

'To keep an eye on the interests of the show.'

'And just what does that mean?'

'To try to anticipate your moves. If someone in his company is involved, to try to save him from surprises.'

'Hasn't he got Cantrell for that?'

'Cantrell's reduced to commanding the palace guard. He's no detective.'

'Also, he's notoriously been no friend of Wayne Larner.'

'I gather he hasn't always watched his tongue,' Kenworthy said. 'He has no room for show-biz in general—or for anyone else who isn't short back and sides. I'm surprised that he took on the job.'

They were climbing a stony track between walled fields. They stopped to lean over a gate, commanding a panorama of limestone scars and tiny rectangular parcels of land, marred by the barbarism of a modern limekiln-complex on the skyline.

'I've been keeping out of your way,' Gleed said, 'so that you could get around in your own fashion. It's time you told me what you've found—apart from Julian Harpur's spikes.'

'The Doncaster connection.'

'What's that?'

Kenworthy told him.

'And now you tell me, Gleed: how far have you got with young Harpur?'

'Nowhere—except for acquiring the nastiest taste in the mouth I've had for many a year. You met Mrs Harpur—'

'Briefly.'

'If there is such a place as the judgement seat, that woman is going to answer for the wreckage of a boy's life. It's not true, of course, that Julian Harpur was ever a genius, but he has the making of a very bright lad, and in present-day technology he could be well up one of the trees in the forest. But whether he's retrievable or not, I wouldn't like to say. We've had a trick-cyclist looking over him at HQ, and he won't say, either. He's supposed to have done himself irreparable brain-damage in an explosion, doing an experiment at home that he'd been warned off at school. But that's as nothing compared with personality derangement.'

'I honestly believe that if I could be left alone with him, I could get at something.'

'We made some progress, but he insisted immovably that the spikes had simply turned up on his workshop bench. And I'm left high and dry. I simply don't know whether to believe him or not.'

'So you won't be holding him?'

'I can't. I've just taken him home. Of course, he'll be watched.'

For the last half-minute a sparrowhawk had been hovering over a clump of last year's dead weeds. It swooped and soared away carrying something. They could not see what its prey was.

'Traffic and Forensic have given us some interesting stuff about the car crash,' Gleed said. 'Of course, it had been raining stair-rods, and came on worse after Larner had left the road. But they found a compression of the mud where he had started to brake. And they drew some useful conclusions about the damage done under the bonnet by the impact. Whatever else you can say about Larner, he was a consummate driver. What we think happened was that the Mommsen girl was waiting up by the wall to wave him down before he ran into the spikes: she may have tried to pick some of them up, but it was too dark and there were too many of them for her to do a thorough job. His engine may have been making a hell of a noise, but he had lost speed up that gradient, and he must have been almost in control again when he skidded, pinned Miss Mommsen against the wall, then pushed her through it and over the edge. The inference is that he came within a split second of not crashing at all. The medics found evidence of mild whiplash.'

'Mild? Not enough to kill him?'

'No. What he ultimately died of were injuries from being beaten about the head. Somebody was evidently waiting near the scene and must have taken him off—probably in a very dazed condition.'

'And could that possibly have been young Harpur?'

'That's something I simply can't answer. Would he have been out of bed and out of the house?'

'Harpur certainly couldn't have transported him far.'

'I'm pretty sure it wasn't Harpur. Harpur's odd, and he's nosy. That's why he loiters. But I believe it's without intent.'

There followed a few seconds' silence. Kenworthy was the first to speak again.

'I've said all along that much turns on who knew that Larner had disimpounded his Lotus. But how the hell did the Mommsen lass know that he was going to come up the hill? She'd been to Manchester for the day, on a fool's errand set up by Furnival so that he could go over her pad. We don't know what time she got back, or who she had the chance to talk to. I've thought a good deal about who knew about that car. And have taken the liberty of setting a young man on it.'

Gleed looked at him with comic oddity.

'Honest Fred Kershaw?'

'The same.'

'Keep me posted. It might save me a chore. And there's another line of thought that you might be working on.'

Three miles away there was a salvo of blasting in the quarry. They saw smoke rise and hang over dead ground.

'We are tempted to assume that the tricks against the Mary Magdalenes came out of the same bag as the attack on Larner. They could be a quite separate issue. But they've all got to be gone into. Who wanted to drive the Magdalenes away so that he could get the part for some woman that he wanted to oblige?'

'Dyer?'

'One has to wonder.'

'Or Jimmy Lindop?'

'You seemed to be getting on well with him just now.'

'I've got him scared. He's hovering on the edge of basic truths—because I hinted that you were quite likely to be pulling him in soon to ask him some awkward questions.'

Gleed rolled his eyes towards the heavens.

'You know, a detective needs to retire. It's the only way he can put himself in a position to get things done. Carry on with the good work, Simon. I look forward to hearing from you from time to time.'

CHAPTER 15

It was a bad morning for Joan Culver. She had fallen out with her father because of one of his table habits, his way of scraping the bottom of his cup on the edge of his saucer when his tea had slopped over. She had been living with him, watching him, unable to do anything about him for too long. And her brother Matthew was home for the morning, and seemed to think it actually funny that his sister had got herself mixed up with stage people. The singer's death was not a reality to him. He did not think of Wayne Larner as a person. He saw him not quite as a caricature, but as a phenomenon created by an abnormal way of life—a name without personality.

So Joan was short-tempered with him, and it amused him to see her furious: the sister who had always been so prim and had always looked contemptuous about his private life.

'By the way, I'm out tonight, taking Sarah to a Country and Western frolic at Foolow. If you happen to be doing any ironing, I fancy that pink shirt I wore last week. I'll make it worth your while.'

It was at that stage that Joan Culver decided to put up with this mode of life no longer. She did not know how she was going to do it, but she had to get away. And it was at that moment of conscious decision that Hajek knocked at the front door.

The producer looked more like a great shambling bear than ever. He was wearing the most voluminous sweater that Joan had ever seen. His trousers looked as if they had done a lifetime of field labour and were tucked into the tops of outsize Wellingtons. He might have been mistaken for one of the outdoor workers on the site except for one thing: the fire in his eyes. And for a man who over the last decade and a half had produced several of the most resounding stage spectaculars in the English tongue, his command of it was lamentable.

'You come back, be Mary Magdalene one more week. You be on stage ten o'clock.'

It did not seem to have occurred to him that there could be any counter-argument.

'We have Madge Oldroyd tape. We have Wayne Larner tape. You know movements, timings. You make pivot for Chorus. You teach new Mary Magdalene when she here. We make contract next week.'

His eyes were scanning her face, cutting like a laser through all it encountered.

'I'll be over,' Joan said. 'Ten o'clock.'

Kenworthy also had a visit. Julian Harpur's father had taken a day off work. He came with his wife to the small apartment that Furnival had put at Kenworthy's disposal at the Hall. The couple had been living on their nerves for two days, and their eyes bore witness to nights awake.

'Mr Kenworthy—where have we gone wrong?'

'You wouldn't much like my answer to that,' Kenworthy said.

'Nevertheless—'

'Then to be brutal—it's taken you too long to ask that question.'

'Mr Kenworthy—we owe you an apology.'

Mrs Harpur murmured keen but not very articulate agreement; she had been allowing her husband to do all the talking so far.

'You see, we *know*, Mr Kenworthy, that he had nothing to do with those spikes. It would be entirely out of character. Oh, I know you'll say that in the state he's in it's absurd to try to make any such claim.'

'We do not believe,' his wife said, 'that the trauma that has thrown him temporarily off-course has interfered with his moral training. We are sure that wherever else we may have failed, our efforts have gone too deep for that.'

How blinkered could people be? Kenworthy expressed no opinion, encouraged them to go on talking.

'Perhaps it would help, Mr Kenworthy, if I went briefly over the nature of the disturbance he has been struggling against. There *may* have been some damage to brain cells, that is as far as the medics are willing to go. Sandra and I are inclined to agree with the psychiatrist, who believes that an aggravated guilt complex is much more likely to lie at the root of the trouble. All that happened was that he carried out a perfectly puerile experiment—well, you can't call it an experiment. He brought chemicals home from the school laboratory after hours. The headmaster, of course, could only see it as a disciplinary offence.'

'He has been wanting for years to treat Julian as a delinquent.'

'And would have done this time, only he'd have had some awkward questions to answer about the security of his stores. Julian's shame was greater than he could bear. He knew that he had behaved childishly, treating science like a toy. He believes that he has betrayed everything he has been taught about absolute values.'

There was only one thing more dangerous than professional psychiatrists—and that was amateur ones. Kenworthy continued to keep his opinions to himself.

'It has been an intolerable burden to him,' Julian's mother said, 'and he has collapsed under the weight of it.'

'And now we learn that he has been wandering about the village and its surroundings at night, when we thought he was reading in bed. And I'm afraid—'

Harpur fidgeted with embarrassment in his chair.

'—There was some trouble with a detective-constable about peeping through actresses' dressing-room windows. And I'm afraid that Julian has something to answer for there.'

'Mind you, these women should not put temptation in men's way. Some of them are very careless about their curtains.'

'But this other thing—these spikes—he would never have been so irresponsible.'

'So you are suggesting that the spikes were planted in your workshop?'

'There can be no other explanation.'

'Have you any concrete reason to suspect it? Any signs of break-in or interference?'

Harpur did not wriggle, but he looked as if it would have been a relief to him to do so. To what extent was he here only to say what his wife had scripted for him?

'Have you noticed any suspicious loitering?'

'I cannot say that we have. We are not detectives, Mr Kenworthy.'

Kenworthy sat back and looked at them for a moment: they were the unbelievable epitome of inconsistency and illogicality.

'I am not clear what you would like me to try to do.'

'To talk to him, Mr Kenworthy. My wife tells me that you were making great progress with him the other day.'

Again, Kenworthy suppressed himself.

'He was talking to you more fluently about his submarine than I have heard him speak for months,' his mother said. 'Please, Mr Kenworthy—we believe that you can get at the truth.'

Another moment's thought.

'I'll have a go—given the opportunity,' Kenworthy said.

Kershaw made the mistake of going straight to the garage proprietor. A more experienced operator would have made his first soundings lower down.

He drew hostile fire. The owner had heard all he wanted to hear about Larner and his bloody car, thank you very much. And Larner or no Larner, he wasn't going to discuss a client's business with an outsider.

Kershaw came away from the sump-oil stink of the office, despondent with failure. But when he was half way across the main workshop, he was buttonholed by a jack-of-all-garage-trades who looked and smelled as if he used sump-oil as sauce on his lunch-plate.

'You the law?'

'You might say that.'

'Couldn't help hearing what you were saying in there. The old man doesn't know which side his bread is buttered, cold-shouldering the law. How much is it worth to you?'

'A fiver.'

'Make it ten.'

'All I want is to know how Larner's car came to be released to him.'

'You've come to the right chap. I was the stupid bugger who released it. Tried to argue with him, first off. But after all, it was his car. And now I'm working off a week's notice.'

'It hadn't been arranged beforehand?'

'It had not. I must have gone soft in the head. I let the ponce talk me into it.'

'You mean *buy* you into it, don't you?'

'Keep your voice down, for God's sake. The boss went spare. He got on the phone straight away to Peak Low Hall. God knows what they said to him. He's hardly spoken to me since.'

That call would have gone first through the switchboard. Who would have been on duty on Saturday afternoon? Kershaw remembered a blonde in Reception who had not cared to be disturbed from a letter she was writing.

Kenworthy did not want it to look as if he considered Julian Harpur his first priority, did not propose to jump at the call of the Harpurs. In any case, it was high time that he had a word with this character Tandy.

Such had been the pressure on accommodation in Peak Low that Tandy had been unable to find anywhere to lay his head in the village. He had to make do with lodgings that people looked on as something of a joke: a bed, a chair and an old whitewood table in a granary on a hill-farm two miles from the village. Kenworthy went on foot. It was a bracing morning, with leaf-shoots beginning to sprout on the hawthorn and a great deal of bird activity in the hedge-rows. As he neared the farm, he saw that a police car was parked outside it, and decided to prolong his walk in some other direction until it had driven off. Then he saw Gleed come out of the house with another officer. He had a second change of mind and hurried towards them.

Gleed laughed at the sight of him.

'Two minds with but a single thought—but I'm afraid our bird's flown. How free are you to come and go from Peak Low, Simon?'

'As free as I care to make myself.'

'Free to go to London?'

'Or Paris, or Tokyo.'

'Because Tandy didn't sleep here last night. Paid off his rent and went off about tea-time, taking all his worldly effects in his banjo-case. From all accounts, he's the sort of Cockney who becomes physically ill if he's out of the Smoke too long. Of course, I'm getting the Met on to him. But you, Simon—looking for characters in London is your métier. And one never knows what priority requests from outside forces are going to get. Besides, this is something that belongs to your vintage, not to today's men.'

'You mean Wayne Larner's early years?'

'The Stalag. The Stalagmites. Izzy Ginsberg. Susan Bistort, if you can find her. I know I have a nerve to ask.'

'I reckon I'd have been on my way by tomorrow at latest.'

CHAPTER 16

Kenworthy walked the Seven Sisters Road in steadily increasing gloom, mostly inspired by the bulldozing passage of time. It always depressed him to contemplate the unrolling of the decades backwards to the end of the war. What made him feel his age was that he did not share with some other people their sharp differentiation between this era and that: between the years of be-bop, skiffle, Carnaby Street, Aldermaston and junkies under Eros. There was a sameness about the post-war years in Kenworthy's memory. Time had simply passed. He could roughly demarcate the phases drawn by the social historians. But when he really wanted to orientate himself, it was to his cases that he looked, to his promotions and his provincial journeys. What had been so very different between the 'fifties and the 'seventies? 1970 was as far away from him now as the First World War had been when he was a kid at elementary school. The New Look, Mods and Rockers, the years of the Teds, were as distant as the gay Nineties had been when he, a fifth-former, had just been elevated to the Second Eleven for his slow off-spinners.

It was no use pretending that he had ever known the Stalag, that he had ever heard of Izzy Ginsberg. But he knew both well enough by prototype: the catchpenny coffee-bar in a dirty basement, the coaxing of money out of inflated adolescent pockets, the decibels amplified to the level of damage to eardrums.

There had been a time when Kenworthy could have dissected anything he wanted to know out of Seven Sisters Road by waiting for it to come to him on a street corner— or by looking for a recognizable elbow on a bar counter. There had been a pub he had always had a soft spot for:

frosted windows, red plush, even Pearly Kings on Saturday
nights. He dropped in there now, and the windows still
looked better suited to a urinal. But the plush had gone,
and the bar was a battery of lagers brewed in the UK and
masquerading behind gothic lettering. Two barmen were
under-employed, and one of them took his time about serving him.

Kenworthy went back into the street. Who had he known
in Holloway and Finsbury Park? Nobby Clarke, who'd done
a few months for illegal possession of transistors. Hell!
Nobby must be in his eighties now. Dodger Allen, who'd
never lost hope of earning half a crown for grassing titbits
three weeks old. Hadn't he picked it up that Dodger had
died of a lung cancer, oh, five years ago? Or was he thinking
of Pete Smalley, taking for his own use a pedal cycle without
the consent of the owner?

Of course, Kenworthy told himself, he could always amble
as far as the nearest blue lamp, see if there was a desk
sergeant old enough for them to have common acquain-
tances. But even desk sergeants these days looked as if they'd
just come out of the sixth form.

A fifty-yard frontage of lock-up shops was missing. The
rubble where they had stood was screened off by wooden
hoardings: a poster (last year's) for a folk-concert, racist
graffiti.

'Mr Kenworthy, sir—'

Five feet four of senior citizen—a chalk-stripe jacket
and a food-stained club tie to which its wearer could not
conceivably be entitled.

'Sorry?'

It was bad not knowing the man, but the Tich was too
cheerful to show disappointment. Kenworthy must have
been a bigger event in his life than he had been in Kenworthy's.

'Go on, sir, you couldn't forget a mug like mine.'

'It wouldn't be for want of trying,' Kenworthy said.

'Billy Jarvis. The Tankersley Gardens business.'

Memory cleared, points coincided, slots slid open.

'Come and have a drink, Billy.'

'On the wagon, Mr Kenworthy.'

'Give me pleasure, watching you down a tomato juice.'

'Makes me feel such a twit.'

'Let's find a pie and peas, then.'

'On a diet.'

'You poor old bugger. You'll be telling me next you've gone straight.'

'That's not very kind, Mr Kenworthy. And they told me you'd retired.'

That of course was something that no one of Billy's vintage could never meaningfully believe. They could not think of Kenworthy as independent, stirring abroad without devious purpose. Billy Jarvis was glad to see him. It was often those to whom Kenworthy had given the roughest time who were the most tickled to see him again.

Kenworthy finally took Billy to a café of Billy's own choice. And they said, times had changed: the shack, the counter, the till, the aproned proprietor—they could all have existed along a stretch of ribbon development in the 'thirties. Kenworthy looked at the dejected cakes nominally protected from flies by sliding panels of smeared glass.

'Have a wad, Billy?'

'One won't hurt, will it? Not supposed to, though.'

'So how's it going, Billy? Evidently somebody's dead keen on keeping you alive.'

The Tankersley Gardens murder had been something less than a mystery. It had been domestic and obvious, except for one untidy cross-trail that had to be cleared. A melancholy innocent had to be exonerated before an upper corridor at the Yard would stop belly-aching. And the man who could give the poor sod an alibi had been Billy Jarvis, whose sole concern had been to divert attention from where he had been himself that evening. Kenworthy had had to run him

in on a petty charge, but had stood up in court with a plea
that he had been most helpful in another case.

'The Stalag, Billy?'

'That's what Jerry used to call PoW camps, isn't it?'

'In one context. This was a dirty little coffee-shop with
jangling guitars. Looked a bit like a cubby-hole in Colditz,
which was why the landlord played it as it was. Izzy
Ginsberg.'

'You mean the Henhouse?'

'The Stalag, Billy.'

'Izzy called his joint the Henhouse.'

'Maybe he'd given it a bit of a whitewash.'

'He had three girls singing there. The Battery Birds. They
didn't last long.'

'Did you ever hear of a group called The Stalagmites?'

'No. But some of these groups only lasted a week or two.
I might have been away on business while they were on the
bill.'

'Or atoning for business.'

'What's *atoning* mean? Mr Kenworthy—I don't like being
got at. I haven't had a hand on my shoulder for ten years.'

'Neither have I. Now—these Stalagmites—'

'Honestly, Mr Kenworthy—you've got me beat.'

'This group had Wayne Larner in it. He made his start
with Izzy, when he was sixteen or seventeen.'

'I know he was Jesus Christ.'

'Temporarily.'

'And got done away with.'

'He served his musical apprenticeship just round the
corner.'

'Everybody knows that. Izzy used to yack on about it, him
being the one that gave the lad his first chance. And never
saw a penny for it, never heard a word of thank-you. Because
this chap came into the caff, can't remember his name,
pulled a face over the coffee, Izzy said—but hoicked the
whole lot of them off at the end of the week. Izzy lost a lot

of trade, being left without music at short notice. Music don't grow on raspberry bushes in the Seven Sisters Road.'

'Exactly. It's The Stalagmites we're talking about now, Billy.'

'I can't remember what they were called. It's all one bloody big noise to me.'

'There was a girl singing with them.'

'Was there? I never went there. Izzy didn't exactly cater for the likes of me.'

'Susan Bistort—that was her stage name. Bickerstaffe, it said on her birth certificate.'

'Right little tart, she'd be.'

'I want to find her, Billy.'

'Mr Kenworthy—I know sod-all about people like that.'

'I know who you could ask.'

'Who's that, then?'

'Alfie Tandy.'

It was clear from Billy's face that the name meant something to him.

'What had Alfie Tandy to do with Wayne Larner, Billy?'

'You know Alfie, Mr Kenworthy. Wasn't it you who did him once for wasting police time? Because he was one of those nutters who go round confessing to crimes that they didn't do?'

'Not me, Billy.'

Nor was it. But Kenworthy knew well enough the flock of cranks and inadequates, the schizos and psychopaths, who would go to any lengths to draw attention to themselves: Lil White, Percy Pople, 'Napoleon' Dean, to mention a few regulars. They made unnecessary work. They cluttered the place up when you wanted space. Somebody had to go through the motions of listening to them, getting it down on paper, filing it—just in case.

'When a geezer got stabbed on a corner of Enkel Street,' Billy said.

'Not my case. What's Alfie ever had to do with any
singers, Billy?'

'He was always hanging round them. Izzy didn't want him
in his place. He never spent anything, and the sight of him
was enough to keep Izzy's regular customers away. And the
group didn't want him either, because he was a pain in the
arse. Well, if you don't know Alfie Tandy, Mr K, you don't
know him. A miserable old bugger, and a bloody know-all at
that. I mean, it wouldn't matter whether it was an electric
guitar or a motorbike engine. Alfie might know sod-all about
it, but he'd tell you how to handle it, if you get me.'

'I get you, Billy. Here—buy yourself some smokes.'

'Had to give them up, Mr Kenworthy.'

'Well, put it in your funeral club. And Billy—Sue Bistort
—Bickerstaffe—I don't know what she calls herself nowadays. She was once married to Wayne Larner, whose real
name as you very well know, was Johnny Lummis. She went
to the Cowell Street Comprehensive with the rest of The
Stalagmites. I want to talk to her. And I'm not here for
long. Tomorrow morning, Billy—here.'

'It'll cost money, Mr Kenworthy. Bus fares—'

'I'll make it worth your while, Billy.'

A man was stabbed on the corner of Enkel Street. Kenworthy remembered. One of Arthur Hurd's cases. Arthur
had retired before Kenworthy had: and now Kenworthy did
have to go to a blue lamp and tell an old comrade story to
pick up his traces. They proved retrievable. Arthur lived in
a semi on the favoured side of Streatham Common.

Kenworthy had never worked with Hurd: they had always
been parallel. But they knew a lot about each other, and
could talk elliptically, in a sort of oral shorthand. No need
for footnotes.

'Stabbing. Enkel Street. Early 'sixties, Arthur.'

'Pub insult.'

'Where did Alf Tandy come into it?'

'Where he always came into things. Trying to reckon he'd
done it—when he hardly bloody knew what had been done.'

'And I believe you nicked him for it.'

That was unusual. It meant a lot of work for a piddling
result. Sometimes you, or a social worker, if you could find
one with the time, would talk a habitual confessor into going
in as a voluntary patient. More often, you made sure he was
truly in the clear and kicked his arse out of it.

'I had to nick him. He wouldn't be satisfied. He was
difficult. Totally unreasonable. When I'd torn his statement
to shreds, he insisted on making another, quite different. I'd
warned him before. So I did him for wasteful employment.
And that meant another court appearance, another day
down the pan. He got a conditional discharge. But the beak
told him he'd go down if he did anything like it again—and
do you know what? That brought an element of realism into
Alfie's life. He never did come that caper again.'

Hurd claimed not to remember much about Tandy, but,
chatting round him, it was remarkable how much came
back to him. Kenworthy picked up more than dead bones.

A war baby, first lot: the result of one of his father's
five-day leaves from France. Nothing known about his early
years, except that they had been in the East End. He had
done dead-end jobs in the 'thirties. Delivering green-
groceries on a bicycle, storeman's toe-rag, boilerman. He
had no form, had been in no kind of trouble until the urge
to confess got into him. He had been in the war—Pioneer
Corps, if Hurd remembered correctly: private soldier, heavy
labour, relaying railway track in France after the invasion.

When he came home, he got hooked on further education
—WEA, LCC evening classes. You mention it, he'd been
to a class about it: current affairs, book-keeping, Roman
London, home loom weaving, appreciation of opera. And
besides Evening Institutes, public libraries had been invented for his special benefit. He had increased his word
power from more first chapters than any other man in

Greater London: Geology, the Royal Houses of Europe, Zen Buddhism.

'He'd learned it all and he'd understood nothing,' Hurd said. 'I remember asking him which books he'd thought worth reading twice. He looked at me as if I was mad. What sort of a nana would want to read the same book twice?'

One detail revived another.

'After the war, he tried to get into the Beefeaters, but for some reason that he never knew and always resented, they turned him down. So he became a night-watchman, a hospital porter, and for a short and stormy spell, a traffic warden.'

'Unmarried?'

'Who'd saddle herself with Alfie? Lived in a YMCA hostel for years. Was in digs when I pinched him.'

So Tandy had ended up in the dock, and they had found a formula to save him from becoming a charge on the tax-payer: a conditional discharge. It was obvious that nobody had ever tried to go into Alfie Tandy in depth. Nobody had ever had time to. Kenworthy said all the right things to Arthur Hurd and spent the night in his own bed.

CHAPTER 17

Kenworthy spent a second night at home, but it was a short one, because he arrived back in London late from a visit to the seaside. The reason for this excursion was the zeal of Billy Jarvis who, perhaps because he did not appreciate the full value of the goods he was delivering, presented his accounting slips with apologies.

'I know 80p seems a lot for buses, Mr Kenworthy, but them's the fares, these days. And I don't think two quid for snacks is out of the way, is it? And I hope you don't mind —I had a half of lager.'

'Thought you were off the hard stuff, Billy.'

Billy had done better than Kenworthy had dared to hope for, but he had not had to be spectacularly clever. There were alumni of the Cowell Street Comprehensive who had not moved all that far from home, among them contemporaries of The Stalagmites. Consequently he had been able to put Kenworthy in touch with Sue Bickerstaffe. (She went under another name these days, but that was irrelevant, and had to do with a marriage that was not a marriage, and that was too complex for Kenworthy to bother to follow.)

Susan Bickerstaffe was one of the most pathetic alcoholics that he had ever encountered. For whereas one of the most notorious characteristics of the addict is the ability to get supplies whatever other shortages there may be in her life, Sue Bickerstaffe had sunk below the means to satisfy her craving. This played into Kenworthy's hands—but it was not a situation that brought him pleasure.

In professional necessity he could adapt himself to most conditions, but he kept returning to the thought that Susan Bickerstaffe might at one time have had more likeable traits: and she was barely yet out of her thirties.

She needed—not wanted—gin, and he took her where there was gin for her to see. He bought her gin—not readily, and at longer intervals than she would have opted for. He hated himself for doing it, and he knew that when the effects of the topping-up had worn off, she was going to be in a worse state than he had found her in.

Her thoughts were in confusion, but she told him things. She told him things that she was contemptuous of him for not knowing. She kept forgetting who he was—if she had ever grasped it in the first place—and he did not try to tell her where his interests really lay.

But she did tell him where Uncle Alf was to be found. Alfie Tandy was no blood relation. Yet he had stayed in touch with her since The Stalagmite days. On the first Friday evening of every month, he took her to a local called The Shipwright's Arms, where he bought her a single glass of Guinness and preached to her about the fecklessness of her way of life. Sometimes she failed—or forgot—to turn up. But Uncle Alf's loyalty went on unperturbed: she was on his duty roster. And he had looked her up since his return from Peak Low.

Alf Tandy proved to be a surprising man. There were facets of his character over which Kenworthy pondered on his long journey back to the North-West. Alf Tandy, knowing that there must be a pack on his heels, was cutting his losses and living his life half a day at a time. He was expecting to be picked up—in fact waiting to be picked up—and he assumed that Kenworthy had come for just that purpose. He had heard of Kenworthy, as had any Londoner of his age and provenance. He did not believe that Kenworthy had retired—or that any copper ever truly did. He professed a great regard for Kenworthy's cleverness and record, and seemed in a quiet way flattered that it was Kenworthy that they had sent to come and get him.

He was resigned to the probability of losing his liberty in his old age, and was unobtrusively enjoying what might well be his last holiday. He had gone to Ramsgate, where he was staying in what must have been one of the least desirable boarding-houses in the town, in a terraced back-street lost in the brick huddle that is known as the Plains of Waterloo, where he was living out of his banjo-case. Here, he told Kenworthy, he had stayed before the war. For one week in every year of his childhood, his parents had brought him here. Kenworthy found him in a public house called The Prussian Eagle, where he was sipping at a milk stout and studying the Stop Press of the day's race meetings. He was wearing a pair of grey flannel trousers, with turn-ups, clearly a legacy of his early manhood. He had on a whitish shirt with an open-neck collar and a dark blue blazer, with a pocket badge worked in the insignia of the Pioneer Corps. His turn-out was completed by a very old, yellowing straw panama, despite the fact that there had been no sun since he had come here and none forecast.

He did not cede the pass to Kenworthy at once. There was a ritual of prevarication in self-defence that had to be worked through first for honour's sake. Kenworthy had work to do, softening him up, showing him that they shared the same attitudes to men and the world, trying to rouse Tandy's sense of humour—in vain, for he had none. But this had always been Kenworthy's strength as an interrogator. He could appear to be on his subject's side. He put Alf Tandy and himself on a common and sympathetic plane, created the illusion of a unified and, unfortunately for mankind, all too rare viewpoint.

So Alfie Tandy went on to tell Kenworthy how things had once been, how he had seen the world developing, and what future he saw for society. And there were moments when there was a catch in Alfie's throat, when his eyes blinked wetly. They went together to a shellfish stall, where Kenworthy had a plate of whelks, and Tandy one of mussels.

'I shan't half suffer for this,' Tandy said. 'I always do when I eat these bloody things.'

'You were a bit of a mug, you know,' Kenworthy said, 'going for Larner with spikes in the road. I'd not been on the ground half an hour before I knew it had to be you.'

'I don't know what you're talking about, Mr Kenworthy. I don't know anything about any spikes in the road.'

'Shall I tell you how I knew it was you, Alfie? It stood out a mile. Because nobody else would have wasted his time like that. Everybody else, from Lord Furnival down to the greenest Tippexologist, knew that Larner was off the road for the duration—or they thought he was. But not you, at your London end. You came steaming up the old Midland Line with a working selection of scrap metal hidden among the smalls in your banjo-case. It didn't take you long to find out your mistake—just as soon as you talked to Jimmy Lindop. Then you suddenly saw your chance, that Saturday night.'

It was the sort of reasoning that deeply impressed Alfie Tandy. Kenworthy had always found that if you could show, even by guesswork, one piece of information that your man had not thought you could possibly have, you were three-quarters there.

Tandy raised doggy eyes into Kenworthy's. Oh, he was a clever bugger, this one was. Always had been.

'That's not how it was, Mr Kenworthy. I'll admit that that's how it nearly happened. But it was not meant to be. That's the only way I can look at it.'

Not meant to be—Like many of his kind, Tandy was not a religious man in the orthodox sense, but there was a strong seam of vestigial belief, sentimental at bottom, that came readily to the surface in any crisis.

'You'd better take me through it a step at a time, Alfie,' Kenworthy said.

'I'll do that, Mr Kenworthy.'

CHAPTER 18

On the train from London to Manchester, Kenworthy read in the early evening edition that there was trouble up at t'mill at Peak Low: a lightning strike of technicians. He did not think that Lindop was actually a shop-steward, but he was likely to have the shop-stewards on tight strings.

Kenworthy went straight up to the Hall, since there would be invidious speculation in high quarters if he went first to see Gleed. Freddy Kershaw was waiting for him in the entrance hall, on one of the settees set at a low table within call of the receptionist's desk. At the sight of Kenworthy, Kershaw nodded goodbye to her, as if they had been enjoying the last half-hour. Then he began to edge Kenworthy out of her earshot, with an almost dramatic insistence on secrecy.

'I've got it, sir—I know how the word got round about Larner's car.'

'Oh yes? Good man.'

'The garage rang, sir. The call was taken at this switchboard. The girl put it through to Cantrell, and within two minutes he was in conference with Furnival. Then they called Dyer in.'

'But how could the word have got through to Miss Mommsen—and perhaps even Tandy?'

'I'm still working on that, sir. I can only think it must have been the blonde, sir, at the desk. It wouldn't be one of the top lot, would it?'

'Wouldn't it?'

There seemed something vacant about Kenworthy, as if he no longer attached much importance to the matter of Larner's car. He turned towards the foot of the stairs.

'Have you offered comfort and succour to Miss Culver?'

'Yes, sir.'

Kenworthy went up the stairs, passed Dyer coming down, and saw an even deeper melancholy than usual in the impresario's face. Something was fermenting inside Dyer, and the venom was distilling into his eyes. It was more than a sulking bout. It was a deep-reaching sickness at the unpalatability of life. He passed close to Kenworthy, but turned his face the other way: a puerile gesture, but he looked as if he were beyond tolerating human society.

Kenworthy tapped on the door of Furnival's sitting-room, which was used as a common room for the inner cabinet of the *Passion*. His Lordship and Cantrell were alone there. Cantrell was on his feet, like a man on a club hearth, and it was evident that the conversation that Kenworthy was interrupting had been, if not heated, energetic and discordant.

'You went a bit far, there, Charles—not that I give two hoots about it. As soon as the legal bods have got the new clauses organized, there's no call for Dyer to stay here. I shall tell him to bobby off. Oh, hullo, Kenworthy. I was beginning to think you had deserted us.'

He was superficially jocular, but there was more than a hint that henceforward Kenworthy's place, unless he wanted to give up the assignment, was in Peak Low.

'Sorry, sir—but I think I've sorted the main thing out. Or, at least, I've broken its back.'

'Oh—you mean the mere murder of a pop star? We're in danger of forgetting about that, Charles and I.'

'You mean labour troubles?'

'Labour? That's a mere pretext. We have a strike on our hands because Szolnok ticked off a lighting man, whereas his writ runs only to sound. Lindop thinks he's got us over a barrel.'

Kenworthy risked provocation.

'He has, hasn't he?'

'Not by industrial action. The money I pay is too good for that. They'll be back at their switchboards and battens tomorrow. Lindop's real object was to demonstrate what could be done. What worries me is his hold on those tapes. He has all the good ones—and God knows how many bad ones. And some of them *are* bad. There are some that go back to the Stalag—and Larner's language on them is worse than Szolnok's and Hajek's. We've every right to burgle his stores, they being my stores, but even if we did that, there's no telling what he's got stashed away elsewhere.'

'Sack him. Get an injunction,' Cantrell said, impatient that Furnival should be considering any other solution.

'And wait for him to tell the great waiting world all that's happening? Let the media and the wholesalers of pirate cassettes know? Be your age, Charles. There must be some way of handling him. And I still say I couldn't have a better man at the console. I don't propose to let him off the hook now, foot-loose and antagonized.'

'I know what I'd do.'

'So do I, Cantrell. And you'd have a deserted theatre up

in these here hills that had never raised its curtain to an audience. Kenworthy, I wish we'd had you here today. I hope you're not thinking of swanning off again tomorrow? Never mind about who killed Larner. Leave that to Gleed.'

'I'll be here, I don't need to make any more outside inquiries.'

'Then give your mind to Lindop. I called you in for your ingenuity, and I need that ingenuity now. By whatever means, I want all Lindop's master-tapes in my own safe-keeping. And I want anything that might harm the show to be bulk-erased and better bulk-erased. And I'm sorry, I'm forgetting myself. We live in troublesome times. What will you drink? I apologize for being so ungracious.'

Kenworthy had no wish to do his talking in front of Cantrell and he indicated this by a flicker of his eyes. Furnival made no ceremony about asking the Colonel to leave them.

'Two bad mistakes I made, Kenworthy. I shouldn't have taken on Lindop, good as he is. Dyer did warn me about him. But I suppose it was one of those things. I wasn't having Dyer calling all the damned tunes. And I shouldn't have appointed Cantrell. The reason was, I wanted someone who can be aggressive in crises. I can be tough when I have to be. But I'll be frank with you: it suits my book to play the easy-going liberal and pay someone else to make himself unpopular. I didn't know then that he hates the guts of the entertainment world. He's just upset Dyer, leading off quite unnecessarily about some of Larner's peccadilloes—as if Dyer needed to be reminded of them. It isn't that I have any sympathy with Dyer. It was in such bad taste—and so childish.'

For a few seconds Furnival put on his good taste act—as if nothing else in the world mattered to him but fastidious behaviour. Kenworthy stretched out his legs luxuriously.

'Cantrell's trouble is personal,' Furnival said. 'A few years ago his daughter, who was eighteen at the time, got involved to some tune with some group or other—nothing to do with anything in Larner's life, or Dyer's. Drug scene. Rescued and persuaded to dry out. Did dry out. Then got hooked again. It's not a new story. And it's surprising how often it happens to people that you and I know, people of standing. Well, there's nothing to be surprised at in that, if you come to think about it. If Cantrell's as reactionary at home as he is about this place, then he might as well be running a forcing-house for drop-outs. All of which ought to have come out in my inquiries before I took the man on. I ought to have called on you to do my positive vetting for me.'

'It's funny,' Kenworthy said. 'Not so very long ago, I was listening to a similar story. On a very different plane, though.'

'Yes—tell me what you've found out.'

'I met a man who candidly admits that he came to Peak Low with the intention of killing Wayne Larner.'

'You mean the little fellow who keeps his spare socks in a musical instrument case? We all thought he'd done it.'

'His scheme didn't work. Larner was too good a driver. But he could tell us who Larner's killer was. He was almost a witness.'

'You've passed this good news on to Gleed, of course?'

'He won't find it good news—only indifferent. Tandy won't talk. I got to know him remarkably well in a very short time. He has a sentimental inhibition about grassing. In fact he has hang-ups, mostly sentimental, about all manner of things. When Tandy says No, it's a waste of time asking him again.'

Kenworthy sat back and let a drop of whisky rest on his tongue.

'I remember a case I had just after the war, when I was leaning on a security suspect in Berlin in 1946. He was one of the few who defeated me—though, of course, everything was loaded on my side—and you'd have thought he had nothing going for him at all. He'd been gun-running against the Allies in Syria, and by some administrative miracle we had a near-perfect file on him. His movements in the Middle East were matched by the visas in his passport. But he beat me by obstinacy. If ever I were in trouble, Lord Furnival, I know what I'd fall back on. Unreason. If you have the nerve to be consistent—and as long as they lay off crude physical stuff—there's no one can crack you. I'd been tackling this bod in bad French —it was the only common ground we had—and his was worse than mine. But when things started getting sticky for him, he simply ceased to understand the language. I tried Arabic through an interpreter—and that gave him a rest while we found one. It worked for a few minutes. Then he gave up understanding Arabic, demanded Turkish. And the same thing with that and various other European languages and desert dialects. We passed him on to a specialized Interrogation Camp where they could produce any lingo in the world, given time. The word I got, months later, was that our friend went on winning—until they found a weakness in his personal background and introduced an element of mental agony. Well—Alfred Tandy is like that Arab. He is unreason triumphant.'

'I hope he'll be treated to a spot of applied psychology as your Arab was.'

'I don't know how Gleed will handle him. I rang Gleed the moment I'd said goodbye to dear Alf. Felt quite a bastard for shopping him. The Kent police have him in transit in this direction at the moment.'

'And you say he knows who the murderer is? You could hazard a guess at a name?'

'No name that I'd care to mention at the moment,' Kenworthy said.

'Now you're being exasperating.'

'What else can I be? Tandy thinks he knows who killed Larner. He dropped colourable hints that it was someone near to the central nervous system of your show. But my suspicions are my own, and if I were to breathe them at the moment, there'd be no telling what action you'd take. And suppose I was wrong?'

'So instead, I have to go around suspecting everyone.'

'A healthy attitude. I hope that's what you're doing already.'

'Well, leave that side of things to Gleed, Kenworthy. I haven't engaged you to do his work for him. Your job is to keep me informed of what's happening: not to try to make it happen. And the only thing that matters to me at the moment is getting Lindop back under control. It's Lindop who has to be your priority. And God knows how you're going to tackle him.'

'In that nebulous region,' Kenworthy said, 'where blackmail and logical persuasion are barely distinguishable.'

'There's no need to make it sound quite so disgusting. Promise me that that is your main endeavour.'

'No problem—the two cases—let's call them the two aspects—are closely related.'

Kenworthy looked at the time.

'I wonder if Lindop's in bed yet.'

'He's not even on the premises, Kenworthy. That's what peeves me. He's ruined a day's rehearsals by pulling out the main labour force—as well as the main fuses. And off he's gone with his Deviants to some pub date in Rotherham.'

Kenworthy grinned.

'I know what Cantrell would do about that.'

'And we both know what Lindop would then do with some of Larner's choicest recordings.'

CHAPTER 19

Kenworthy had made no haste to leave Furnival, and it was consequently very late before he was able to telephone Gleed, which he did from the public kiosk in the Peak Low Square. Gleed was in bed, reading the same page he had read every night for the past week. Kenworthy had not spoken to the Detective-Superintendent since he had rung him from Ramsgate to deliver Tandy into the hands of his transit captors.

'I've seen Furnival and told him as much as it's good for him to know. I had no more than a word with Cantrell. He appears to have upset Dyer. Dyer cut me dead on the stairs, but I don't think there was anything personal in it. I think Dyer's had more than enough.'

'So you'll be ready for a night's repose?'

'No. I cat-slumbered in the train. I want to talk to Lindop while he's still weary from today. Dyer and Cantrell can wait till the morning.'

'They'll get here with Tandy sometime during the night. We've told the Press a man's being brought here to help: no names. I shall go straight over and weigh in.'

'You'll not break Alf Tandy with words.'

'I've got to try, though, haven't I? Be in touch in the morning. And good luck with Lindop. By the way, I've had Fewter and Nall working all day on that crate of theatrical equipment that was delivered into the theatre under your eyes and Furnival's, the morning Hajek lost his cool. I'm pretty sure that that's how Larner's corpse was brought in. But they came up with nothing—so categorically nothing that I'm sure I'm on the right track. The van can't be traced. The driver and his mate can't be traced. We even found the so-called delivery note that Hajek screwed up and threw down in the stalls. And that was something that must have been picked up from where the wind had blown it. It was an invoice for a prefabricated henhouse that was delivered in the village last week.'

'The theatre is patrolled at night, I take it?'

'By Cantrell's men.'

'I'm thinking about when the crate can have been unpacked and the body transferred.' Kenworthy said. 'It can only have been by night.'

Kenworthy rang off. He knew that he had an hour or two in front of him. If The Deviants had a pub engagement it was unlikely that they would leave the premises at closing time. The night could be advanced before they fetched up back in Peak Low. So Kenworthy went up to the Hall unhurriedly on foot. It was between three and four o'clock when he heard on the hill an engine that he diagnosed as a minibus. He moved into a convenient shadow when he saw where they were going to park. He was not near enough to differentiate properly between the personalities: two men, two women, one of whom might be old enough, to judge from his movements, to be of Stalagmite vintage. They had musical instruments in cases. Lindop was the fifth member of the party and had heavy equipment, including speakers. Kenworthy heard him say that he was going to leave most of his stuff locked in the van until morning: there were just a few things that he was not going to allow out of his possession. His stock of compromising tapes, for a certainty. Did he take them to bed with him?

The two couples had reached the main entrance to the Hall while Lindop was still fiddling about at the vehicle. He was leaning in at the rear door, unaware that anyone was behind him, when Kenworthy touched his back. He swung round, ready for anything, the edge of his right hand poised for a kung-fu chop. Kenworthy raised a warning hand.

'Spare me, Lindop. I need to talk to you.'

'Not tonight, you don't.'

'We'll keep it short.'

'Here and now, then. Not one minute more than five. Shall we get into the van?'

'Upstairs in your quarters, I think.'

'That means you'll be there half the night.'

'I'm just back from seeing Alfie Tandy,' Kenworthy said. 'And Sue Bistort into the bargain.'

'Where the devil did you unearth her—and why?'

'Alfie had looked her up, the moment he got back to the
Smoke. Very attentive to Sue Bistort, is Alfie. He seems to
be a pretty faithful type, when he takes someone under his
wing.'

'Faithful? Yes—that's one word you could use. OK, then.
Curiosity doth make idiots of us all.'

Lindop's room, not surprisingly, was an overflow workshop: a light work-bench, tape splicers, a bank of high-fi re-
production panels, and everywhere magnetic tape of all
calibres in every conceivable form of cassette and container.

'Shall I percolate? Or would you prefer usquebaugh?'

'Percolate, please. As you guessed—we may not conclude
this immediately.'

'I was afraid not. Unless I conclude it by dropping off.'

'I don't think you will,' Kenworthy said. 'I think you'll
be very wide awake in a minute or two.'

Lindop looked at him with burlesque expectancy.

'Well?'

'Well, you can do me a favour for a start. Lord Furnival
is getting a little crotchety over my dilatory ways. So put
me in a position to tell him I've actually done something
he's asked me to.'

'What's that?'

'Give into my safe-keeping two stacks of tapes, clearly
labelled *model Larner*—and *far from model Larner*.'

Lindop laughed.

'And you think there's some slight grain of hope that I'd
agree to that? I couldn't, in any case. The stuff has never
been properly logged and labelled. I've never got round to
indexing it. That's one reason.'

'And the other?'

'You're not going to spoil the best bit of fun I've had since
I was taken to my first pantomime.'

'I think I'm going to change your mind for you within
the next quarter of an hour, Lindop.'

Lindop pulled one of his repertoire of funny faces—the

one that said that he was prepared to hear any man out, provided he didn't repeat himself too often.

'I told you I'd seen Susan Bistort.'

'Poor old Snakeweed. How was she? I'll bet she didn't ask after me.'

'No. She wasn't really interested in asking after anyone. In fact, protracted conversation on any single topic was a bit of a strain on her—and on me.'

'Poor old Snakey!'

'Anything behind the nickname?'

'Bistort—Snakeweed—two names for the same plant. A weed. We'd learned *Bistort* in Nature Study and chose it as her stage-name. It sort of followed from Bickerstaffe. Then our biology teacher, the sarcastic cowson, saw her name on the board outside the Stalag and christened her Snakeweed in class.'

'She's in a bad way.'

'No need to tell me that. There was a time when I might have got steamed up about it. One more down to Larner.'

'But you've cooled off about her?'

'Yes and no. I'm not sure that it's fair to blame every damned thing on Larner. Snakeweed was perfectly capable of going wrong in her own right.'

Kenworthy drank coffee, set his cup down on a minimally vacant table-corner.

'You mean you're no longer in love with her?'

Lindop looked at him in surprise at first, then for a second as if his come-back might be short-tempered. Then he made another face.

'Not since I was seventeen.'

'At which time all The Stalagmites were in love with her?'

'Ah, but I was the only one who loved her for the sake of her beautiful soul.'

'And what put you off?'

'She married Larner.'

'And since they split up?'

'I've not come across her much. I saw her once when I was back in London. I saw what the liquor was doing to her. I saw what she was having to do to pay for it. And I didn't fancy having to finance her. It didn't make me feel any more kindly disposed towards Larner.'

'You weren't tempted to try and take her in hand?'

'I was never that much of an optimist. What are you getting at, Kenworthy?'

'I just wondered.'

'Well, I'll tell you the truth. I found her revolting. Make sure that goes into your notes.'

'OK. Forget her. She was too woolly-minded to know what she was doing or saying, but she did put me on the road to Alfie Tandy. And also for my notes, Lindop, I want to know precisely what he had against Larner. He did tell me, but I need to know how much to believe. I gather he had a nephew.'

'Barney Chisholm. Alfie's sister's child, brought up by Alfie's mum. Barney was percussion and vocals—not that we ever let him do a solo. And he wasn't all that clever on the drums. He couldn't maintain a tempo for two bars at a stretch. And in the soulful passages, he sounded as if he was knocking up a henhouse. Believe me, Kenworthy, The Stalagmites were bad. But none of the others was as bad as Barney. We had to put up with him because Alfie was grub-staking us.'

'Who else was in the group? Anyone else who stayed in that kind of music?'

'Only Ed Manterfield. He's with The Deviants. He's learned a few things since the Seven Sisters Road. I think if The Deviants can only get a disc out of this show—'

'Let's get back to young Barney.'

'We had to put up with him. We needed Alfie's shekels. But like us all, Barney was stranded when Dyer pinched Larner. We were sacked from the dance-hall at Stockwell where Dyer had first put us. Izzy Ginsberg wouldn't have

us back. And you've got to understand this about The
Stalagmites, Kenworthy—rotten as we were, all we lived
for was what we were doing. Now we'd no lead singer, no
lead guitar, no Snakeweed, because she went along with
Larner in his early days. We broke up. I went to the Tech.
Barney followed a lamentably common course. Too much
drink, too many joints, from pot to LSD, got truly hooked,
vanished from his normal circles—until he turned up in a
temporary nick they'd put up at a pop festival. He died in
that nick—of just about everything: drug overdose, alcoholic
poisoning, septic arm from a dirty needle, malnutrition and
backhanders across the mouth from the fuzz who busted
him.'

'Lucky to be identified, wasn't he? Was he with pals?'

'He had no pals. He had his name tattooed on his arm.
And that's where Alfred began his long pilgrimage as the
agent of Nemesis.'

'Alfie was quite frank with me about it,' Kenworthy said.
'He made no effort to deny intent.'

'He wouldn't. There was always something childishly
honest about Alfred. He'd spent a good deal of his life being
honest about going to kill Larner.'

'He had it all planned, too, didn't he—those confessions?'

'Kenworthy, you can't possibly, in a short time, have got
to know Alf Tandy the way we knew him. When Alfie got
an idea in his head, it was there. He was stuck with it—and
so was everybody round him. He did have the germ of an
idea, sometimes, but like everything else he had it was
half-baked. But any brainwave he had got the full treat-
ment.'

Lindop was a confident arbiter of other men's conduct.

'And there was nothing as half-baked as his scheme to
get known as a compulsive confessor. You've dug that up,
obviously. His idea was to join the confession gang for a few
years. He'd get his arse kicked out of every murder inquiry
he could make his way into. So when he confessed to a

murder he *had* done, he'd be likewise shot out on his neck. Crack-brained? Pure Tandy. And it seems he went too far, as usual. He really peeved one of your oppos, and got done for some kind of obstruction. They warned him that next time, he'd find himself doing bird. And that was writing on the wall in poster paint for Alfie. He didn't fancy going inside. He'd too many outdoor interests. He pulled out of confessing.'

'Tandy was very honest with me, Lindop. I've said that before, I know, but it was striking. It was like having honesty shot at you from a sawn-off shotgun. He spent the inside of his lifetime anticipating the moment when he was going to kill Larner. Isn't that what the philosophers call existentialism? Giving yourself a reason for living? He didn't put it in those words—but that's what he meant. And he got as far as strewing his spikes in the road—but they didn't do the job for him. Larner came blasting up Brackdale Hill, throttle wide open—sending macho messages back to Joan Culver. But he hadn't much speed towards the top of the gradient, and when Ricarda Mommsen came out of the shadows, signalling him to stop, he succeeded in braking—though not before he'd pushed her through the wall. I shall never forget Alfie's face, over a glass of milk stout, while he was telling me this.'

Nor would he. In The Prussian Eagle, in the unseasidely Plains of Waterloo in Ramsgate, Alfie Tandy had leaned across the table, his forearms parallel in front of him. He had talked in toneless Cockney vowels, in the ponderous language nourished by a lifetime of evening classes.

'When he saw I'd arrived in Peak Low, Mr Kenworthy, it must have crossed his mind that I was going to kill him.'

'I can't understand why you didn't kill him years ago,' Kenworthy had said.

'If I tell you, will you believe me? The thought of killing Johnny Lummis has kept me going for years. It was when they made him Jesus Christ that I knew it had to be soon.'

Kenworthy put something into the telling of it, and Lindop was not unimpressed. But it took him by surprise to see the extent of Kenworthy's involvement.

'It was Alfie who spread those spikes in the road, but they didn't kill Larner. And Alfie was waiting round the corner with a gun in his hand, just in case a *coup de grâce* was needed. But he couldn't pull the trigger. After all those years of dedication, he still couldn't do it. His finger wouldn't put that final pressure on. But he knows who was waiting to beat Larner about the head—because he saw who else was out and about on that stretch of road. All he'd say then was that it was someone close to the top people. Though I saw it myself, Lindop, I'm not without experience of persuading people to tell me things they hadn't intended to tell me. But I know no way of getting facts out of Alfie Tandy that he wants to keep to himself. I even believe that physical torture would be counter-productive.'

'It would get you nowhere,' Lindop said. 'I've seen Alfie Tandy with his heels dug in. Beyond a certain point, the man has no sense. And that's a strength in itself, when one's opponent is a man of normal standards.'

'I know.'

Kenworthy told Lindop the story of the Arab gun-runner.

'So I can understand why my one-time colleague Arthur Hurd lost his temper with him. In my opinion, his whole concept was illogical, anyway.'

'In what sense?'

'Why save all his bile for Wayne Larner? Wouldn't the more obvious target have been Dyer?'

'Not to Alfie's way of thinking.'

'Why not?'

'Because Alfie had never put money and effort into Dyer. Dyer wasn't family. And Alfie looked on The Stalagmites as his own flesh and blood. He had put money and effort into us—though he wasn't all that popular with us, you know, despite all we owed him.'

'But to your way of thinking?'

'My way of thinking?'

'Wouldn't you have settled for killing Dyer, if you'd been Alfie Tandy?'

'I've never considered killing anyone,' Lindop said, and he said it with crisp emphasis.

'Not even wishfully?'

'Why should I? I've led my own life. I think I can claim not to have failed on my own pitch.'

There followed a short silence and Kenworthy seemed disinclined to be the one to break it.

'So what happens now?' Lindop asked him.

'Alfie is being brought here. To help. He's probably arriving just about now. Of course, you and I know how helpful he's going to be. And the other thing that's going to happen is that you, Lindop, are going to hand me two sets of tapes.'

'And if I did, how would you know how much back-up stuff I'd kept in reserve? Do you have to spoil this for me, Kenworthy? I promise you I'm not going to bugger up any public performance. Damn it, I have some loyalty to showbiz—I have to live by it. But don't you see—Furnival is like Alfie Tandy's Wayne Larner, wondering if and when Alfie Tandy is going to kill him. Furnival's just waiting for it to happen—the wrecking stroke. I've got tapes of Larner: tapes of Larner drunk, tapes of Larner high, tapes of Larner obscene, Larner singing *The Good Ship Venus*. I've even got an early taped rehearsal of The Stalagmites. How would that sound on the Mount of Olives? Furnival daren't sack me. What security would it bring him, knowing I'm running wild?'

'He won't be sacking you, Lindop—nor will you be running wild. The only thing I could get out of Tandy was that the identity of the murderer will shake the top people. So where does that put you? Aren't you the obvious man to be framed? Oh, I know you have an alibi for Saturday night

—but that won't stop them getting you as an accomplice. The stunts you've been involved in—and you know what I'm talking about—I wouldn't put it past them proving that you masterminded the whole shoot. I tell you, I know which way Gleed's mind is working. I can see you going down, Lindop. Yesterday, you used the word *vulnerable*. Do you appreciate just how vulnerable you are?'

'So how does it help if I hand over the tapes? I can see it helps *you*—'

'It's time you made an honest man of yourself, Lindop. So you've got Furnival over a barrel. And where does that put you next year—and the year after? Stop fooling about, man. Get rid of everything that puts you on the wrong side —and let it be seen that you've got rid of it. Go and talk openly to Gleed—about the Mary Magdalenes for one thing.'

'You make it sound like sense, Kenworthy—and I'm never too happy when a man in your position appears to be talking sense. It needs thinking about. I've always been a loner. I was a loner in the Stalagmite days.'

'You'll be a loner if you find yourself banned from every sound console in the country.'

'I'm not making my mind up here and now, in your presence, Kenworthy. When a man's had an idea in his head for years—'

'He stands every chance of ending up like Alfie Tandy.'

The thought obviously startled Lindop, but he remained stubborn.

'That almost does it. But I'm going to walk all round it again.'

'Well, don't take too long. You're going to be a watched man.'

CHAPTER 20

The troubled quiet of a hospital at night is a muffled micro-cosm of the human condition at a pathetic extreme: a distant fan, here a groan, there a cough, a delirious obsession, a repeated phrase that means nothing except to the man who has it on his mind.

Gleed had rostered three women officers to invigilate by Ricarda Mommsen's bed, and they reacted in contrasting manners.

Sonia Saye, 10.0 p.m. to 6.0 a.m., was bored beyond toleration: another long downhill chute away from her deter-mination to make a career in the Force. The paperback on her lap advanced only a page or two at each session. The atmosphere—for Sonia—killed concentration. She wanted to be where there was a different kind of action. And there was no sort of empathy between herself and the muttering, murmuring, unlovely woman for whom nobody could do anything except with drip-feed and sponge.

Dorothy Purvis, the afternoon shift, was more interested in the thrown-up by-plots of the ward than in a vegetable-woman with whom she could not communicate. There were a few of the nurses who occasionally tried, whispering a word or two close to the unresponding features, as if it were clinically desirable to penetrate into her consciousness. The more experienced neither believed nor disbelieved that she might ever be rehabilitated. Everybody was waiting.

Kate Seymour—everybody called her Jane, though it was not her baptismal name—was on duty the night Ricarda Mommsen spoke a line of verse. Death had visited the ward earlier in the evening: curtains drawn round a bed against the opposite wall; cardiac arrest, oxygen cylinders, the ulti-mate failure of the resuscitatory drills. Then trivialities

loomed important. The staff nurse was trimming the finger-
nails of the cadaver before the next of kin arrived.

Ricarda Mommsen was restless, more restless than usual.
Jane Seymour had looked for hours at the ugly yet strangely
sensitive face. She felt she knew the patient intimately, every
twitch and tremor, without knowing the most elementary
thing about her. She desperately wanted to get into the mind
of this woman, wanted to know—and not just for the case
report.

'Staff!'

Jane called Staff Nurse Bentham over.

'She's talking more tonight. She's trying to get something
out.'

The staff nurse leaned down close with her ear. 'Sorry.
Can't help. It sounds like German. Means nothing to me.'

'Nor me. But I do have this.'

Jane Seymour laid a pocket-size recorder down by
Ricarda Mommsen's pillow.

'*Gib mir die Hand*—'

A huge physical effort. And so near to the English cognate
words that anyone could understand it.

'—*und komm*—'

No difficulty there, either.

'*Wir werden sie uns pflücken gehen*—'

That defeated Jane. And so did the last line, a passionate
whisper after a considerable pause.

'*Sie werden wohl die letzten sein.*'

Ricarda Mommsen died about twenty minutes later without saying anything else articulate.

Gleed tried through every local linguist that he knew of to
get the quotation identified, but it was not within the capacity
of anyone within his reach. It was only next day, when he
ordered a full search of the few possessions in Miss
Mommsen's room, that they found the poem, marked in an
anthology. It was from Cäsar Flaischlen, a turn of the century
symbolist poet, picking the last roses of the season with the

implication that there were no more seasons to come.

Jane reported personally to Gleed, who had asked to see her, since she was the last person to hear anything at all from Ricarda Mommsen's lips. The Superintendent had Kenworthy in his office with him, a character whom all Gleed's minions found enigmatic.

'It isn't like this in books, is it?' Kenworthy said. 'It would be a rotten story that ended, *We shall never know.*'

'Well, we shan't,' Gleed said. 'I suppose some women are capable of her kind of loving—especially a woman with a tradition of persecution in her very bloodstream.'

'I think she was very conscious of that. She knew—she must have known—how wretchedly Larner had treated her. Literally, one night of love—and only because, in the true Larner tradition, she was so unlovable that she appealed to his devious vanity. Then he dropped her—but she didn't drop him. If she hadn't lost her life signalling to him that night, maybe he'd have lost his a little earlier than he did. And we still don't know how she found out what Alfie Tandy was planning.'

CHAPTER 21

'Twelve degrees right.'

'Obstruction. I'll bring her back, start again.'

Kenworthy, lying painfully on his side on a bed of loose stones, was trying to prompt from Julian Harpur's notes with one arm crushed against the wall. What one would endure to try to prove a theory!'

Opportunism: he had seen Julian Harpur leaving the village, carrying his now completed submarine.

'Need any help?'

Harpur's reaction had been to glower as if he resented being spoken to.

'She's in full working order now, is she?'

Harpur's grunt said yes—but wished that Kenworthy would go away.

'I'd like to see you put her through her paces.'

The outcome was that Kenworthy was now dictating from Harpur's notes while the youth set the boat at the task that obsessed him. Meeting House Dale was not one of the Wonders of the High Peak. It was not more than a shallow cleft in the steep hillside in which one of Peak Low's Nonconformist chapels nestled. And what Julian Harpur had called a water-swallow was no show cave. More properly he should have called it a rock-shelter—not much more than the entrance to a cave not yet formed. But it did swallow water —the agglomerated trickles of several hill-springs, and that water ran away into the furthest extremity of the opening, suggesting the possibility of a more developed system of water-courses within. But as the channel through which the rivulet entered the rock was not more than nine inches high, there could be no thought of human exploration. Young Harpur was anxious to chart this channel, and he hoped to do it by plotting precisely the course on which he steered his submarine. He became relatively talkative about it.

'Nobody knows where the water goes, see? They've tried dyes, but no one has ever seen coloured water come out anywhere.'

He was not in a friendly mood, and was deeply absorbed in controlling his craft. He did not appear to hold a very high opinion of Kenworthy's brain, and clearly doubted his ability to carry out the simple instructions he had given him. And for his part, Kenworthy had to admit that he was anything but clear about the boy's calculations. It seemed to be a clear case of delusions of grandeur. Harpur was convinced that he was about to make an exclusive scientific discovery.

The climax came after about an hour, when he lost radio contact with his model. After increasingly feverish activity, he had to admit that he had lost his submarine too. There was little likelihood that he would ever get it back. Kenworthy felt sorry for him, but it was a sympathy offset by the fury of the boy's reaction, which harked back to the emotional responses of infancy: he blamed Kenworthy because it had happened. This was not the way that Kenworthy had wanted the afternoon to develop.

'You know, one of these days, Julian, you're going to come up against someone who's just not prepared to put up with the way you carry on.'

Kenworthy could not have predicted the effect of this very carefully controlled rebuke. Harpur's attitude changed. He seemed to try to take a grip on himself. But this did not turn him at once into a civilized being: he sulked.

'You know, I'm expecting to be here for several days, and there are any number of things I'd like you to show me. But how can you expect anyone to want your company if you can't be consistent for ten minutes together?'

Harpur looked as if he were on the verge of crying. He was a case of protracted infancy. Kenworthy decided to go for the main chance at once.

'I don't care for people who tell me lies, either.'

Harpur looked at him as if he were unaware of what offence he might have committed now.

'Those iron spikes that I picked up from your work-bench. You told me that someone must have been in and left them there. But I know now where you got them from.'

Harpur looked as if he feared drastic reprisals.

'And I do happen to know why you didn't want to tell me the truth. You do know that I used to be a detective, don't you? And there's nothing magic in being a detective —but it did teach me to look at the patterns of things. I always look at patterns, Julian—and ask myself what they can teach me.'

Harpur was beginning to be curious about what he was getting at.

'I had a good look at your house last time I passed it, and I worked out which must be your bedroom window. The one with the Boeing B-17B on the sill? So I had no difficulty in spotting which drainpipe you come down by. Did you know that your weight has loosened one of the brackets? It's beginning to come away from the wall. And I could see where you put one foot on the top edge of the water-butt to jump down to the ground. Do you know there's a concavity beginning to show in the rim?'

Harpur was now showing apprehension.

'Oh, don't think that I blame you. You're big enough and old enough to be allowed out alone. If you were my son, you wouldn't have to climb out, because I wouldn't mind if you were out. I'd trust you. But what I'm coming to is this: you didn't tell the truth about those spikes because you didn't want anyone to know that you were out of the house after midnight on Saturday.'

Harpur's response was the sort of silence that is an admission of guilt in mature criminals, as well as wayward children.

'I'm right, am I, in assuming that you picked up those spikes up Brackdale Hill, not very long after they had been put down?'

'Only three,' Harpur said.

'So did you see who put them down?'

'M'm.'

'Who was it?'

But Harpur could only shrug.

'Can you describe him?'

'He always carries a guitar about with him.'

'I know the man. It isn't a guitar—it's a banjo.'

'He had the spikes in the case.'

'I guessed as much. Now listen, Julian. This is important, because it will help me to work out what happened. Where were you at the actual moment when this man—his name's Tandy, by the way—was scattering the horrible things?

What I mean is, how come he didn't see you?'

'There are bushes at the side of the road. I was behind one of them. And it was dark.'

'So you saw the car—the Lotus—crash?'

'M'm.'

'And the driver wasn't hurt?'

'He got out. He looked drunk.'

'How could you see him on such a dark night?'

'The man Tandy had a torch.'

'So what did the driver do next?'

'He walked up the road.'

'He joined Tandy?'

'I don't know. I didn't see him again. The torch had gone out.'

'Was there anyone else about at the top of Brackdale Hill?'

'There was a woman. I don't know her name. She tried to stop the car—the first car.'

'The first car?'

'The Lotus. There was another car, coming down the hill. It stopped before it got to the crash and Wayne Larner got in it.'

'Julian—I'd like you to come with me to Brackdale Hill now. I want to know exactly where people were standing, where they were hiding—and any other possible hiding places that there might be. Because places have patterns that tell me things. I expect you've read Sherlock Holmes?'

The boy nodded.

'Well, I don't pretend I'm as clever as he was—but wherever any man has been, he leaves something. The question always is, is it something you can see?'

So they went back to Brackdale, but while they were still some way off the site of the crash, it was obvious from parked cars and a group of men that activity was going on. Fewter and Nall, with a couple of juniors, were engaged in a field exercise—searching the wooded side of the road, and obviously trying to establish key-points at the top edge of the ravine. As soon as he recognized them, Kenworthy tried to withdraw Harpur and himself away from them, but he was too late. Fewter had spotted them, and beckoned.

'I see you've got yourself a new assistant.'

'And a very helpful one too,' Kenworthy said. 'We've just had a very useful little talk.'

'We talked to him for forty-eight hours.'

Harpur was beginning to hang back.

'Show this gentleman exactly where you were standing when the car came up the hill, Julian.'

Reluctantly, Harpur showed them a clump of brushwood about five yards back from the road. Kenworthy went and stood there, taking good care to register how much of the road the position commanded.

'Now show us where Mr Tandy waited.'

Harpur walked back several yards and pointed to a rising contour where all manner of weeds had taken possession of a broken wall.

'And Miss Mommsen?'

She had waited twenty yards lower down, on what would have been Larner's near side. So she must have dashed across to the wall when she heard his engine.

'Are you suggesting,' Fewter said, 'that this youngster was out and about and up here last Saturday night?'

'You just heard what he said.'

'It's not what he had to say before.'

Fewter turned his irascibility direct on Harpur.

'You've got some explaining to do—and some written statements to retract. Superintendent Gleed is going to love you.'

Harpur looked covertly at Kenworthy for protection.

'Just what you were doing out of doors at that time of night?'

'He wasn't breaking the laws of the land,' Kenworthy said.

'I'm asking *him*.'

'Well, I wouldn't, if I were you. I don't know his reasons, but I suspect they are perfectly legal—and personally embarrassing. And what are you going to get out of him if you rub him up the wrong way?'

'I think you've retired, haven't you, Kenworthy? Would you like to retire from this conversation, too?'

CHAPTER 22

When Joan Culver's brother settled on an idea, it was difficult to dislodge it, and repetition never seemed to weary him. This morning he kept on about her foolhardiness in continuing as a temporary Mary Magdalene. He was overwhelmed by what the Press was saying: the cheaper papers were making a major news item of her.

VILLAGE GIRL COCKS SNOOK AT JOKER—JOAN UNJOLTED.

No threat by stage-side vandals is strong enough to weaken the pull of the footlights for pretty Joan Culver—

She was annoyed when a group of excitable journalists came to the back door while she was in the middle of clearing the breakfast things.

'Are you really going to go through with this, Miss Culver?'

'Are you hoping that they'll give you the full part after all this?'

'May we quote you as saying—?'

She could not stop them pressing through the door. She blinked at their electronic flashes, did as they asked when they wanted her to pose with her back to the kitchen sink.

And they crowded round her all the way to the theatre. Did she believe that the joker had anything in store for her this morning? Didn't she find it off-putting, trying to act with a cordon of Cantrell's security toughs all round her? And always there was the suggestion that her heart was set on stardom. One of the dailies had come up with the story —totally false—that she had always been overlooked in school plays, and had promised herself that she would make it to neon-lights one day.

Then Cantrell's watch-dogs were barring their way from following her any deeper into the inner sanctums of the theatre, and she was in the quiet corridor outside the dressing-rooms, already agreeably familiar to her.

The scene that Hajek was hoping to start pulling together today was the women's dawn walk to the Sepulchre to annoint the body of their friend and master. According to the scriptwriter, Mary Magdalene had been the instigator and leader of this expedition. The other women—Joanna and the sisters Mary and Martha from Bethany—were older than she was, and frightened of every shadow that edged their route. Mary Magdalene was nervous too, her tension breaking through at the leap of a cat. But she had to put courage into the others as they walked between the ancient walls, waiting for the gates to be opened at sunrise. They were ordinary women, doing what they believed in, trying to ignore the dangers that they saw and felt. The walls of Jerusalem were projected on a screen behind them. The music, predominantly electronic, was full of atmosphere. 'You know,' Furnival said to Kenworthy in the body of the auditorium, 'what I like about the New Testament are these episodes that touch off reality. You get the feeling that they could not have been invented. And this one—what those women did and said that morning—that has always clinched matters for me.'

And what effect had that had on his life? Kenworthy did not bother to ask. On stage, the women were all set to go.

But Hajek risked puncturing their readiness by calling them forward to the apron and repeating their briefing.

'OK? OK, Sound? OK, Lights?'

It was not Jimmy Lindop, but one of his assistants at the audio-panel this morning.

A chord from Szolnok, and Joan began her opening aria. *Oh, who shall roll away the stone?* She was resolved that this time her voice should not sound weak—or if it did, then a brand of conquered timorousness should be the hallmark of Mary Magdalene. But Hajek was restless after the first few bars.

'Never mind the song. Move on from the last line. Play us the coda, Szolnok.'

He was treating his musical colleague with excogitated courtesy. This sometimes happened between the two when the demands of the show took on primary importance.

Joan felt flattened: her pivoted presence on the stage was no more than a convenience to Hajek. It was difficult to maintain an illusion in the face of this kind of deflation. But then suddenly the lighting was dimmed to the first nuances of a reluctant dawn—the merest slash of slightly pinkish grey in the blackness over a crenellated city fortification. Some new menace rustled in the shadows of a house door-way. But it turned out to be only a bundle of old rags, blown a yard and a half across the cobbles. A cat sprang—and with it, it was to be hoped—every pulse in the stalls. A configuration in a minor key from a synthetic *vox humana* insinuated the women's terror of the next corner. They reached the manned gate in the outer wall, and the captain of guard looked as if he had a mind to challenge them, but he was too idle. There were itinerant merchants outside the walls, waiting to come in, and the women were forced off the roadway to make way for their lethargic loaded camels. Then there was squalor beyond the city boundaries, the filth of a Middle Eastern rubbish tip at the dawn of an era. For a quarter of a mile they had to pick their way over ordure and through shadows, the sunrise still little more than obscurity.

A bucket of refuse narrowly missed them, thrown over the city wall on their left hand. Joan Culver was gripped by the role that she was playing. She *was* Mary Magdalene, and the women she had persuaded to come with her were losing heart, Martha of Bethany already lagging, a fifty-year-old, past physical fitness, so that they had to let her set the pace. And there was some other fear in the air, something even greater than the conventionally macabre. It was fear of the unknown, of some pending event that they could not yet conceive, the feeling that within the next few minutes they would come upon something inexplicable and intolerable.

Joan Culver turned on her heel and the women moved from left to right behind her. The filmed background took them along another enclave in the ramparts. Joan Culver suddenly screamed—and it was not a scream from Mary Magdalene: it was a scream from Joan Culver.

'Cut! Cut! Cut! What the hell now?'

'I'm sorry, Mr Hajek. There was somebody here—somebody real.'

Feet scurried away, behind a canvas flat.

'A stage-hand—What the hell? When are we going to do this scene in one piece?'

'No, Mr Hajek—it was not a stage-hand.'

While the Road to the Sepulchre was being rehearsed. Gleed, Fewter and Nall were in conference. Gleed was not at his most patient. He was taking them—he hoped for the last time—through their report on the delivery of the crate in which Larner's body must have been brought into the wings.

'You've established that it was a dirty white Bedford van with no contractor's name on the side—'

'But discoloration where a previous owner's name had been painted out. Illegible.'

'Dozens of people must have seen it—but no one noticed the registration.'

'No one. Why should anyone? People don't go about noting car numbers.'

'You questioned the whole village, more or less. No one saw the vehicle come in?'

'Why should anyone? Vans are coming and going all day. This one was doing nothing out of the ordinary.'

'No one even happened to notice which direction it came from?'

'From the angle at which it approached the theatre, we assume that it came from the Manchester road, north of the village. Ninety-five per cent of traffic here comes from that road.'

'And the delivery men?'

'Looked like delivery men. Faces not known to anyone in Peak Low or in the Show.'

'And nobody started to unpack it?'

'As far as we can see, it was addressed to no one. No one took it as his responsibility. Lights thought it belonged to Scenery, Scenery thought it was meant for Props.'

'So we're back to the original assumption that it was unpacked at night.'

'It must have been.'

'And Cantrell's mobile patrols are supposed to have been making snap checks all night?'

'Yes—and if their logs are correct, that's what they were doing. And those timings show that the corpse must have been unloaded between two and three in the morning.'

'How efficient are these patrols?' Gleed asked.

'I think they were slack at one time, but Cantrell has tightened things up since Larner's crash.'

'So whoever unpacked the corpse must have taken chances. Unless he knew the movements of the patrol in advance. Are they scheduled—or random?'

'Scheduled. With random variations.'

'So someone may have been in cahoots with the patrol.'

'I'm dead sure someone was,' Fewter said. 'Somebody must have been in cahoots with somebody else, somewhere along the line. How hard have we to carry on looking for that van?'

'We haven't the manpower to give it priority. Keep your eyes and ears open. We can hardly do more than that.'

When Kenworthy went back to his apartment after Joan Culver's burst of hysteria, he found that a large and heavy cardboard carton had been delivered to him. It was filled with magnetic recording tapes of all makes and sizes.

You'll find they're not logged. Hard work for someone, finding out what's where. Sorry I can give you nothing stronger than my word that this is the whole collection. I hope that this will be interpreted in the right quarters as an act of good faith. I am pulling out—permanently. I hate admitting you're right, but there's too much ill-will about here. No doubt someone will come trying to find me. A waste of somebody's time.

JL

CHAPTER 23

Freddy Kershaw ran a G registration Morris Minor, an obvious object of bathos after the Lotus. Joan laughed at the racket of an engine that had topped 150,000 miles. It was a laugh that said a number of difficult things, things that it would be far better not to try to say in ordinary words. Freddy had been to see her once before, and conversation had been like crossing a dark room known to be littered with broken glass. Now he had turned up unexpectedly to suggest a change of scene and a meal out: to take her out of herself, to break the pattern—that kind of rationalization. To his surprise, she did not produce any counter-rationalizations. He drove them up into gritstone country. The tappets rattled on gradients. Great tracts of country opened themselves up, around and below them. They ate at an unfrequented pub. Joan found Freddy's bearing different from Wayne's. His attitude to waitresses was different. He lacked Wayne's urbanity, but he was more restful than Wayne, more reminiscent of her own kind. She felt as if she had been exiled from her own kind for a very long time. Yet it was only last weekend that she had branched out experimentally for a matter of hours.

'Freddy—what is happening?'

There were, of course, village rumours. Joan had heard only snatches. Since Saturday, people had tended to drop their voices when they thought she was within listening range.

Freddy Kershaw had heard rumours, too, but had heard no more confidences from Kenworthy; and such members of the Force as he had managed to get to talk to had been lower than policy-makers. Last night he had ventured into a pub where he knew that he might meet men of his own vintage coming off duty. He did come across a few, and they made him feel as if he no longer belonged, as if an æon had passed since he had been one of them. But a man with whom he had done his initial training had drifted into talk with him, though only minutes ago he had been treating him as vaguely hostile. So Freddy did at least pick up what theories were being canvassed on the perimeter of informed circles.

'They seem to have been holding this man Tandy for a long time now, don't they?' Joan asked him. 'And it was given out on the news this morning that they have charged no one yet. What's holding things up?'

'The buzz is that Tandy knows something—that he saw someone up in Brackdale on Saturday night. He reckons it's someone near the top. But he's holding out—a stubborn man.'

'Near the top? You mean one of the producers? Hajek? I

know he's temperamental. He's had a lot to put up with. But he surely wouldn't go so far as to—'

'Hajek? You'll be suspecting Szolnok next. But then, why not? At this stage of a case, everybody's suspect. I've heard nothing official, but it seems that it's the upper few that all eyes are on.'

'Even Lord Furnival and his friends?'

'They do rather a lot of this sort of thing in the circles I used to move in—casting people in criminal roles. Let's find six good reasons why Furnival might want to murder Wayne Larner.'

'Why one earth should he? Wayne was the keystone of his show.'

'His voice was—and they've still got his voice, haven't they? And his charisma. That word's been used a lot in Peak Low in the last few weeks. Larner's voice is his charisma—thanks to the technicians.'

'Couldn't you possibly bring yourself to use his Christian name?' Joan said.

'I don't want to make too much of this, Joan. I hesitate to mention it at all. But there were times when Wayne Larner was an embarrassment to the play. It must have plagued Furnival.'

'But what did he ever *do*?'

'It's the old one about Cæsar's wife. The lead in a religious show has to be above gossip. And Larner came with a reputation.'

'An unfair one.'

'The justice of it isn't relevant. There'd been a nasty business in Nottingham, ten years ago. And there's been talk here. Honestly, Joan—I'd rather not go into detail.'

'I wish you would, please. I'd like to know what detail people think there is.'

'There was the girl who was playing the daughter of Jairus. And then one of the chorus of angels. And then Ricarda Mommsen—'

'Then me, I suppose?'

'Joan—you went shopping with him in Buxton on a Saturday afternoon. He took you for a ride round Cheshire and a meal. That's all it amounted to.'

'No. That was not all.'

'What do you mean?'

She had decided to tell him, had decided not to tell him, had vacillated again, had come down, she thought finally, on the side of not telling him. And here she was, blurting it out.

The Badminton Hotel—the essence of Buxton's heyday gentility, a harking back to the era of the Palm Lounge string trio. It was the first time in her life that she had been through those revolving doors.

'Don't they turn people away if they arrive without luggage?' she asked Wayne, remembering that from some novel.

'Are you kidding? What century are we living in?'

'Never mind what century. We're in Buxton.'

'You've not been around much, have you?'

'Hardly at all.'

'It's not too late to put that right.'

Blue and gold *putti* clung to clouds on domed ceilings; murals portrayed the Pavilion Promenade and the Pump Room. And there were living throw-backs to the period: a hall porter who looked like a combination of regimental sergeant-major and kirk elder. The residents' lounge must surely enshrine the last word in moral censoriousness. Wayne Larner had obviously been here before. He was known and expected at Reception. Then they were following a key-carrying porter to the lift. She knew that she was going to have to talk her way out of this, but she went up with Wayne because she had not the nerve to protest under the eyes of the guests in the foyer.

It was not a room, it was a suite. The porter tested the radiator with his hand, showed them the bathroom and the bedroom. He was too old a hand to give a knowing look—

but that seemed to make him all the more knowing. Their windows overlooked a car park, and the rain was sheeting across it. Joan stood and looked out until the porter had left them. The wooded hills on the rim of the town's bowl were almost totally eclipsed by heavy cloud.

Then Wayne came to her, put an arm round her shoulders and kissed her. She had been kissed before—but never as a frank statement of hungry intent. She told herself that she was not a prude. She could be unconventional if she wanted to. She could throw to the winds everybody's code but her own—when the time came. But the time had not come in this hotel with Wayne Larner.

She gave him back only token acquiescence, released herself as quickly as she could on the not unreasonable grounds that he was crushing her ribs.

'What's the matter?'

She tried to make something of a joke of it, to escape amiably if he would let her.

'I don't think I'm specially delicate. But I am breakable. Besides—'

'Besides?'

'Besides, Wayne—I shouldn't have let us come here.'

'Rather be out in the rain, would you?'

'No, but we don't know each other, do we?'

'I know a good way of putting that right.'

'Wayne—please understand.'

The truth sank in on him.

'You're one of those, are you?'

He was a man blind to everything but the frustration of the moment.

'I'm sorry, Wayne.'

'What did you think we were coming here for?'

'I didn't know we were coming here.'

'You thought we were coming to Buxton to paddle in the puddles, did you?'

She was not far from tears. He partially relented, but it

was with a shrug rather than a smile. He recited one of Max Miller's jingles.

> I like the girls who do,
> I can take the girls who don't,
> I hate the girl who says she will,
> And then she says she won't—

'I'm sorry, Wayne.'

He switched the piped radio from channel to channel, switched off again.

'What did you think we were going to do?' he said.

'We didn't know the weather was going to be so foul, for one thing. I thought there'd be somewhere we could go and talk—to get to know each other.'

'I say again—there's one sure way of doing that.'

'That doesn't come *first*, Wayne.'

'It does with some people.'

'Do all the girls you know look at things that way?'

He appeared to give some sort of thought to the question.

'Yeah,' he said at last. 'Yeah. Maybe you've got a point.'

'Wayne—I'm not saying I'd *never*—'

What was she telling him now?

'But it would have to be with someone I knew—someone I knew I could love. And that doesn't come all at once, does it?'

'You take things too seriously,' he said.

'That isn't necessarily harmful.'

'So what do you want to do now?' he asked sulkily.

'Let's talk for a bit.'

'OK then—talk.'

Not the most fruitful opening for a duologue. But she did talk. She started asking him questions about his mode of life. And he perked up. Talking about himself was no burden.

'Then he told me about them not letting him use his car, and as I told you before, I encouraged him to go to the garage.'

Her cheeks were red. Freddy's reaction seemed no more than embarrassment and confusion.

'You took a risk going into that hotel with him,' he said.

He still looked on her as a young innocent. There was another story—but she did not propose to tell him that one: Llandudno, three years ago. She had gone for a fortnight's holiday with two girls she had been at school with. They were man-mad, and Joan had found a man, too, a business type—so he looked and said. She had slept with him, the last night but one. As an experience on any level, it had been a failure. The next day he had been offhand with her. She had written to him when she got home, but weeks later her letter came back from the post office: the address he had given her did not exist. She told herself she had to forget the incident: there were plenty of men about who would not behave like that. But she could not get it out of her mind. But she knew that she must not tell Freddy.

The sweet trolley arrived, and she went into delight about the gateau. She had such moments of brittle gaiety, when she remembered to force them on herself.

'I know how you feel,' Freddy said. 'But you've got to try to put Wayne Larner out of your mind, Joan.'

'How can you expect me to do that? Freddy, he meant nothing more to me than a singer I was nuts about when I was too young to know any better. But the man's dead. How can I forget him? There are too many things I can't forget. Like making an ass of myself on the stage—'

Her shriek of terror—because there had been a man lurking behind the mock-up Sepulchre. A man? A boy— a lout—that young Harpur. Leering at her—practically *drooling*. She had made such a fool of herself that they had not continued with the scene. Hajek had contemptuously got on with something else. He had not asked Joan to help

out again. It was rumoured that a new—and permanent—
Mary Magdalene was on the way.

'And never mind my troubles, Freddy. You have enough
of your own. If I hadn't asked you to get me my bag—'

'You didn't ask me to get it.'

'As good as. What will they do to you, Freddy?'

'I don't know.'

'Is there any chance that they might reinstate you?'

'Probably not. I'm not even sure that I want them to. I'm
going to play it by ear. It depends on whether they treat me
as an adult.'

CHAPTER 24

'So?'

Gleed squared up a stack of pro formas—nothing more
romantic or sinister than overtime sheets.

'You've inspired a few useful leaks?'

'I've scattered a few crumbs. Appetites varied.'

'Did you learn anything?'

Kenworthy said he thought the exercise had been useful.
It had been Gleed's idea, but it had clearly been better for
someone outside the Force to handle the deception that
Kenworthy had just put over. It had been a question
of letting unauthorized persons know this afternoon's
plans.

'I dropped hints round Furnival's table first. He's my
employer, so he has the right to expect it. But he didn't
behave quite as expected.'

'Perhaps he thought you were spilling the beans a little
too easily.'

'It wasn't that. I really don't think he was interested. He
didn't seem to want to know.'

'That's my reading of Furnival all along the line. A master

of the art of seeming not to do things. I've never seen Furnival in action. He's a man who gets his own way, down to the last detail—yet I've never seen or heard him insist on anything. And I've never heard of him punishing a backslider.'

'I first met him in the army,' Kenworthy said. 'He had a staff appointment at a rear HQ: a penthouse office. He had to have everything spelled out twice over for him. He never seemed to understand a thing that was happening—or to care. That was all a pose. His job was sending men out on tasks from which he knew they wouldn't come back.'

'I fancy it's always wartime for Furnival—when he wants something. He fights his wars with a quiet smile on his face. What about Dyer?'

'Even less obliging than Furnival. Dyer didn't even seem to take any of it in: showed no interest at all.'

'Being subtle, you think? Or a case of bad hamming?'

'I'm tempted to think it was Dyer being Dyer. I wouldn't put much money on Dyer's staying out of the shrink's hands much longer.'

'I think that Dyer had become afflicted by the insipidity of life in general. Or by his conscience.'

'I think Dyer's conscience is a faithful servant. He's used to keeping it in order.'

'So you think the man on his tail is going to have an easy run?'

'I'd make sure he stays on his tail, all the same.'

'That leaves Cantrell.'

'A very different proposition. He really did want to know. "Do you mind if I take notes?—" and pulled the gag about what men like himself have to learn from professionals. I had to do a spot of hard preaching to make sure he doesn't hang about too openly and give the game away. Oh, and you'll be grateful to know that he's offered to lend you a few of his security mobsters, in case you're short on manpower.'

Gleed stood up from his desk, flexed his shoulders.

'You know, Simon—I'd rather like it to be Cantrell.'

'And I'd like it to be Furnival.'

'This dialogue would sound good on *Panorama,* wouldn't it?'

'We're a couple of bad buggers,' Kenworthy said.

'I don't know about a couple. If you hadn't been here, I probably wouldn't have taken a step outside the manual. And Lindop's been behaving in a very interesting fashion. I've had a shadow on him every yard since he left the site. A very tired man, from all appearances.'

'He can't have had much sleep.'

'Well, he really did leave Peak Low. He thought he gave my man the slip—which the officer was crafty enough to let him go on thinking. He drove as far as Bakewell, parked in the public car park outside the police station. Then he did a bit of double-shuffling in and out of a pub, slipped into a garage and hired himself a car on an impeccable credit card. Drove back into the hills with his hatbrim down and his coat collar up. The last report was that he was lying doggo in a lane behind Little Longstone. Which means that he intends to come back—and could be here in under half an hour.'

'Let's hope he's played the game with those tapes—and I think he will have done. Furnival can manage without him now. Lindop's work is done: that was producing the master-tapes. So Furnival's got all he bargained and paid for.'

'He wins again, in fact.'

Gleed looked at his watch.

'Final briefing session in twenty minutes. I can't ask you to sit in.'

'I'd lose my credibility if I did. And I'd better go and rally round his lordship. Who are you putting on his heels, by the way?'

'A face no one knows round here—like all but one that I'm using. A detective-sergeant from Clay Cross. If ordinary

Derbyshire villains knew what strength I've called in from corners of the county, they'd have a bonanza. I'm setting one of my DI's on Dyer—a wily sod called Hewitt who's been beefing about being on an inside job for the last six months. I'm putting a multiple team on Cantrell—he's likely to be mobile, with his squad of watchmen to organize. And on Tandy himself, I'm using local talent: the egregious Sergeant Nall.'

'You don't think he'll try to do the job from inside The Devonshire Arms?'

'If he hasn't learned anything from a few unkind things I said to him yesterday, he's ineducable. Watching Tandy is going to need someone who knows every rock, wall and spinney—just in case he gets lost. I'd have liked young Kershaw on that job—but he's strictly not available.'

'I know. Pity. I'd have liked him on my wing.'

Gleed looked at him like a man who was not going to press one particular question too forcefully.

'Yes—just how do you propose to comport yourself, Simon?'

'Oh, coming and going,' Kenworthy said. 'Hither and thither.'

Freddy Kershaw was kept for a long time in an ante-room while the panel conferred. He had expected them to be solemn men, but he had been surprised by how uninformative their solemnity had been. One of them had looked sour, one bored. Then they asked him to wait. There was nothing in their waiting-room for him to look at, and he had not thought of bringing anything to read.

According to the partially informed, a good deal would turn on whether Ricarda Mommsen had received fatal injuries before the car had actually pushed her through the wall. The inquest had been adjourned, so the pathologist's report was not public knowledge, but there was no lack of soothsayers who claimed to know what was in it. Some said that Ricarda's spine had been broken against the coping while Larner was still braking. Freddy Kershaw had heard a woman scream while the car was still hurtling down. But the panel did not dwell on any of this. They were judging Kershaw on the foreseeable consequences of his actions, not on the luck of the draw.

But what had disturbed him most was the counter-productivity of his honesty. He had expected face-value credit for his truthfulness. Some of the panel, on the other hand, had looked deviously for motives, even at this stage. And, obviously, some of them thought they had found something.

He had been frank with them: Joan Culver had pointed out that her bag was still in the glove compartment. He had judged that he could retrieve it without disturbing the car. A steely-haired superintendent looked at him with eyes that understood only one sort of truth.

'You hoped that by removing this bag, you might be able to hide the fact that Miss Culver had been in Mr Larner's car at all. Wasn't that what was uppermost in your mind?'

Freddy Kershaw was stung.

'No, sir.'

'You wanted to obliterate from your own mind the fact that she had been out with him.'

'*No,* sir.'

Too forceful. Over-emphasis. Self-condemnatory.

'But something like that had occurred to you?'

'Sir—why should that bother me?' he asked. 'It was common knowledge that Miss Culver had gone out with Wayne Larner. I myself had seen them arrive at my billet together. How could I hope to maintain such a fiction as you are suggesting?'

'Detective-Constable Kershaw, we are not here to develop hypotheses. I put it to you that you were in a pretty grim frame of mind as you started up that hill.'

'That isn't true, sir.'

And yet it was. He'd been jealous, bloody-minded.

Then came the ante-penultimate moment when he was given his last chance to add to his evidence. Kershaw had rehearsed a good deal that had been of little use to him because of the way the questioning had gone. And there had been one angle that he had not intended to bring up. It would only be construed as vindictive. He even thought them capable of looking on him as a sneak. In any case, he wasn't out for anyone's blood. Yet he heard his voice plunging on.

'It seems to me, sir, that I would not be here today if I had shown no respect for the truth. If I had done as certain persons suggested I did.'

'*Certain persons*—who are these *certain persons?* Do you propose to tell us? If you are prepared to be explicit, then we shall record and consider your statement. But we cannot listen to anonymous insinuations. Inexperienced though you are, I would have expected you to have known that.'

'I understand that, sir. I mean that my DI and my detective-sergeant wanted me to revise the statement I had made.'

'Your DI did? What did he actually say to you?'

There was nothing for it but to admit that no words were actually used. Fewter's words—or alleged words—had been conveyed to him by Nall. That was hearsay, unacceptable. He had to leave them with the impression that he was as ignorant of procedure as that.

'Wait in the outer room, Detective-Constable Kershaw.'

'So the two-faced sod tried to shop me,' Nall said, trying to enlist Sergeant Wardle's sympathy in the Peak Low police house. Wardle's sole contribution to the affair had been his self-exonerating insistence that he had told Kershaw not to touch the car.

'Damn it, all I told him was for his own good, seeing that he hadn't the bloody sense to see it for himself. The way he seems to have put it to them, it makes it look as if I was giving him orders to tell lies.'

A sour bubble of breakfast bacon-fat dislodged itself from the upper reaches of Nall's digestive tract.

'The silly young bugger even tried to involve Fewter—as if bloody Fewter ever carried a can for anyone in his life. So Fewter's gunning for me too. Christ! Is that the time? I was supposed to be at Gleed's briefing five minutes ago.'

CHAPTER 25

Kenworthy had inconspicuously taken post behind one of the pillars of the auditorium, though without any cloak and dagger show. He could see that one of Gleed's henchmen was already at his start-line. The detective-sergeant from Clay Cross, whose target was Furnival, was in one of the aisle seats, eight rows back, watching the rehearsal. Furnival was also watching it: *The Road to Emmaus*, one of the appearances of Jesus to his friends after the crucifixion. *But their eyes were beholden that they should not see him.*

Until today it had seemed a reasonable link-scene, as well as a convenient way of clearing the depth of the stage for the glorious technology of the Ascension. The original schema had been for the silhouette of Larner's retreating back to accompany the apostles against a projected background of stony road. He was to remain unrecognized until he began to hum a reprise of *There was a shout about my ears* (melody Szolnok, lyric Chesterton).

But the scene was playing worse than flatly. There was something amiss that was worse than the physical absence of Larner. Furnival was chafing and the man in the seat next to him, one of his cohort of scriptwriters, was catching his lordship's full frontal onslaught.

'It won't do. When they see this, it's Larner's death the audience will be dwelling on.'

'Couldn't we omit the sequence altogether?' the script-writer asked.

'Unthinkable. We would be liable under the Trades Descriptions Act. We have promised an unabridged version.'

Dyer was not in the theatre. Why should he be? His sole reason for remaining in Peak Low had been to protect his interest in Larner—and to try to snaffle any vacant parts for others of his protégés. But a contract for a new Mary Magdalene had been signed behind his back, dissipating his last hopes.

Cantrell was not here, either. There was plenty for him to do, checking the deployment of his storm troops. Everything was happening in an altogether desultory fashion. Hajek was in silent mood, watching the acting without comment, though now and then he wrote down a note.

And Szolnok was equally passive. In theory, Kenworthy was no xenophobe. But he was always having to fend off the temptation to turn into a dyed-in the wool reactionary. It was one of the hazards of the policeman's way of life. He had seen many an otherwise fair-minded officer succumb to it. Foreigners—and æsthetes—they had codes that were not as other men's were.

Kenworthy slipped out of the auditorium. *Hither and thither* he had told Gleed his sphere of action lay.

There was a peculiar diversion in the village while *The Road to Emmaus* was drifting through its lifeless lines. A lorry piled cumbersomely with scrap metal had shed its load at the nodal Peak Low crossroads, blocking egress and ingress by three of the four main routes. Sergeant Wardle had come plodding out to make leisurely notes of all the appropriate infringements, and every man, woman and child with time on their hands had gathered to share the excitement.

This operation had been mounted with some degree of

uncertainty since, unlike the *Passion,* perfectionist rehearsal had been impossible. It was Gleed who had laid it on, preferring not to have an audience for the reconstruction of crime that he proposed to mount up Brackdale. Since the exercise was going to involve a wild drive up the hill in a Panda car pretending to be a Lotus, spectators could have made the scene untidy.

It was a small and assorted group of plainclothes officers that Gleed had with him *in situ*—the star player was undoubtedly Alfie Tandy, who had been brought up to show them exactly where he had concealed himself on the lethal Saturday. A woman officer, not looking as if she was wholly enjoying her part, had been told to stand where Ricarda Mommsen had taken the impact of the car. The party deployed themselves and they heard the Panda start out from the Square, roaring up the lower stretch of the hill.

It was remarkable how the wildfire news spread about Peak Low.

In the theatre, it was backstage that the word was passed that this time Gleed really had surpassed himself. He had actually planned to drive full tilt at one of his own women officers up Brackdale, and everybody had been so damned scared that Tandy—who was going to have been charged with murder later this afternoon—had made himself scarce into the backwoods while pursuit was being made doubly difficult by the traffic snarl-up in the village centre.

The word was brought on-stage by the first actor with an entrance to make. So now the action, already moribund, petered out altogether for seconds. Hajek was at last stirred to wrath.

'Now what goes on?'

Someone stepped up-stage and shouted the news down to him. Furnival did not do anything straight away. He waited until the dialogue had picked up again, then said something to his captive scriptwriter, got up and walked without apparent haste towards the main exit. The detective-sergeant from Clay Cross also got up and left the theatre, in his case by a side-entrance. He went out like a man of leisure—but as soon as he was outside, he stepped out briskly along a route that he had already mapped out for himself. In less than half a minute he had Furnival in sight again, and fell in behind him at his lordship's pace.

It was a mobile team that Gleed had briefed to stand by for whatever moves Cantrell might make. During the run-up period, until the action proper started, one man equipped with a personal radio was keeping track of the Colonel's whereabouts.

There had been something strange about his conduct all day. At first it had simply looked as if he were going the rounds checking on his sentries. But it was not long before it became evident that something other than a normal master-and-man relationship was governing his conversations with his old soldiers.

Sergeant Cook, the first fingertip of the watch-force, was unable to approach near enough to hear what their talk was about. Gleed had impressed upon him that Cantrell must not know that he was being shadowed: what mattered to Gleed was where Cantrell made for when he heard that Tandy was on the run.

It looked to Cook very much as if it was the rank and file who were calling the tune in these conversations with their so-called boss. There was nothing military—or even respectful—in their bearing when they spoke to him: hands in pockets, cigarettes alight, even at their duty-points. And it was equally clear that Cantrell was not enjoying himself. He was obviously trying to make some emphatic point, and it stood out a mile that he was having little success. Men interrupted him before he had finished what he was trying to say, and there was more than one occasion when they were all talking at once.

Then they were joined by a newcomer who came striding across a field. Sergeant Cook guessed that this was the crucial messenger. There was no doubt that the news disturbed Cantrell. Whatever the nature of the rift between him and his work-force, there was no doubt that the news of Tandy's escape had shaken them all.

Cook made sure that he was masked by the bole of a substantial tree, pulled out the aerial of his pocket transmitter and reported to Gleed that Cantrell was striding in the direction of Peak Low Hall, at intervals almost breaking into the indignity of a run.

Detective-Inspector Hewitt had been grumbling for weeks about the office-job to which he had been seconded. When Gleed had called him out to keep watch on Dyer, he had sarcastically remarked that he was surprised that he was considered up to it.

And then he came to the early conclusion that he would be lucky if this assignment gave him anything to do at all. For all the signs were that Dyer was packing up to leave, and that he would have the dust of Peak Low off his shoes before the morning was over.

DI Hewitt had gained entrance to the Hall by pretending to be a heating engineer attending to the valves and air-locks of the radiators. He knew that provided he looked authoritative and busy enough, anyone who saw him was likely to assume that his visit was in order. He was even able to enter Dyer's own room, in Dyer's presence—and Dyer's radiator appeared to be giving him prolonged difficulty. Dyer had been packing files into a tea-chest, and had just tied the last cord. Inspector Hewitt bled air from a valve with the special key with which he had equipped himself. He was still in Dyer's room when Cantrell came racing up the stairs.

'Those idiots have let Tandy give them the slip. He's at large in the neighbourhood.'

'No concern of mine,' Dyer said. 'I've nobody else under contract. I'm through.'

Cantrell looked anxiously over his shoulder at the man in overalls who had just noisily dropped a spanner.

'You did have last Saturday night. You'd do better to stick around a day or two, Dyer. We may have to consult. We need to be in close touch.'

At that moment Dyer's internal telephone rang. Hewitt had no difficulty in gathering that the man at the other end was Furnival.

'Yes, sir. Cantrell's with me. We'll be up straight away.'

CHAPTER 26

By the time they took Alf Tandy up Brackdale for the re-enactment, he had had enough. They had tried everything they knew on him and some of the sequences, longish ones, had been anything but friendly. Tandy was a man of character—if that is the word to use of his system, which was to adhere, come what may, to whatever plan of action he had settled on. Only once in his life had he been untrue to a plan conceived, and that had been when he had withdrawn from the confessors' squad. He was still not sure whether that had been a mistake. Since he had talked to Kenworthy at Ramsgate, he had stuck to a simple line: he had seen something, that Saturday night; it had involved someone close to the top. It was one of Tandy's weaknesses that he liked people to know when he was on to something big. He did not give secrets away, but he liked his immediate associates to know when he knew a secret. No one had been able to shake him out of these grooves. Now and then, when they were varying their routines with an hour or so of the *nice guy* routine, he had allowed himself to chat to them amiably, then as soon as they got back to Saturday night, he limpeted up. But the fact of the matter was that even Tandy was beginning to feel a bit jaded. Sometimes Gleed deputed the interrogation to a subordinate, and some of the junior officers lacked the Chief Inspector's patience. Sooner or later, someone was going to lose his temper and hit Alfie. Alfie could feel it coming, and he did not reckon it.

And now the mad buggers had stuck one of their own female officers up against the wall, and they were going to drive a police car at her. What the hell did they think that was going to tell them?

Another thing that they did not know about was Alfie's friendship with Miss Mommsen. Nothing sexy, of course, but there had been something about the Jewish girl that appealed to Alf. Her family had suffered at the hands of the Nazis—and Alfie had fought the Nazis, albeit a hundred miles behind the lines, laying railway metals. Several times in Alfie's life he had taken some young woman under his protection. Snakeweed had been one of them.

Ricarda Mommsen had been stood up by Wayne Larner, so he had thought it a good idea to recruit her as an ally in some of the tricks that Jimmy Lindop and company were playing. And Ricarda Mommsen had not discouraged him. She had not promised her support in any of the capers— but she had listened. She was a good listener, and perhaps Alf Tandy had let fall from time to time more than he had meant to. Because he felt sorry for Miss Mommsen in more ways than one. She fascinated him. Maybe in spite of the gaps and differences he was even a little in love with her— in Tandy fashion.

He wondered now, thinking it over, whether she had talked to him, listened to him, because she was using him, pumping him, trying to get him to give secrets away. Like on that Saturday night, when they had come back from Buxton together on the last bus, and she had tried to wheedle out of him what it was he had in his banjo-case. Because he had let it be known that he had something in there—

something that he was going to play the biggest trick of all
on Larner with. He had not told her that it was iron spikes.
But he had told her that Larner was out in his sports car—
and was going to regret it. That was all of the secret that
he had given away, but perhaps Ricarda Mommsen had
somehow put two and two together. Perhaps she had thought
that it was high explosive that he meant to put down on the
road. So she had not gone home to the Hall. She had come
back and lain in wait to warn Larner.

And now the crazy buggers were trying to do the same
thing with one of their own kind. Tandy saw the woman,
pale-faced and obedient, standing where Ricarda had stood
waving. And then he also saw that everyone was concentrat-
ing so fiercely on this act that they had forgotten him.

Behind him was a belt of trees, and behind the trees hills
and fields—country into which he had not penetrated, had
had no wish to penetrate. He moved a step or two away
from where they had told him to stand: nobody noticed. He
marked out a potential dash from cover to cover: behind
that tree, then sideways behind that one, then down into
the dip, then round the end of that clump of bushes.

Tandy was no master of fieldcraft, though he considered
himself a crafty man—a man would have to get up very
early in the morning to put one over on Alf Tandy. Boiled
down to their basics, Tandy's talents were two: he could
never forget any simple lesson whose wisdom had initially
appealed to him; and he was obstinate. And as far as
movement about hostile country was concerned, he remembered what he had been taught in his army recruit days
about keeping his head down.

He could see that the hinterland of Brackdale was hostile
country. His only possible plan was to make his way to some
relatively habited place from which he could find transport
back to London. Only in London could he see any hope of
concealing himself. To get back to civilization he could not
avoid crossing hills with skylines. He had to risk being

pounced on by some farmer for trespassing. He had to watch that he did not snap brittle twigs under foot or rustle long grasses. And every time he did break a twig or swish against a clump of grass, he halted and looked furtively all round him. It was not long before he was in a sorry state of nerves.

He had a poor sense of direction, and when he passed a decrepit stone barn for the second time, he was forced to admit that he was wearing himself out to no purpose. In front of him loomed a steep hill from the top of which, he told himself, he would be able to see the lie of the land all round, so that he could find a village or perhaps a small town. And then he knew that his troubles would be only starting, because they would be on the watch for him. Yet he started climbing that hill, concluded after five breathless minutes that he was exposing himself too dangerously, decided to go down again and follow the line of a wall up a kinder gradient. He had followed that wall for more than fifty yards when a human figure leaped at him from a rocky hollow. Tandy did not know the man's name, but he remembered him as one of the less amenable ones who had taken over the questioning when Gleed was not there.

At the beginning of the exercise, Gleed had told Nall more home truths in three minutes than the sergeant had heard about himself in the last ten years. It was a long time since anyone had shaken Nall, especially with words.

'Perhaps your memory goes back further than mine does, Sergeant Nall. There must have been some time in your history when you were doing a decent job of work. There must be something in your record to justify three stripes. I'll tell you this, my friend—it's only because I'm short of hands and feet that I'm employing you at all this afternoon. If you fall down this time, I shall have your stripes. And if you ask me if I'm threatening you, the answer is I'm doing my damnedest to make myself clear. Am I coming anywhere near doing so?'

Nall resented it. There was too much truth in it—as sound a reason for resentment as any. It had all started when that idle bastard Fewter got the division. What could that make anybody, but a cynic? Nall also knew that he could not afford to fall down this afternoon. Which was why, he told himself, he was being a bigger bloody idiot than ever by playing his hunch and leaping out at Tandy.

Well, hell—when you were on the ground, you had to play things the way they turned out. You had to use *some* bloody initiative. That was why they'd given you three stripes in the first place. Not that there'd be much future in saying any of this to Gleed if the thing turned sour on him now.

But you couldn't go on stalking this dithering sodding imbecile, wandering in frigging circles till nightfall. You'd wear your sodding self out, plus there was every chance of losing the daft bugger, which would have you deeper up Shit Creek than you were already.

'All right, mate. You're nicked.'

Wholly outside instructions—but play it as it came. Before Nall got Tandy back to HQ, he was going to get out of him all they needed to know. Failure now was unthinkable. Shit or bust.

It was shit or bust for Tandy, too. The little Cockney turned and ran—or turned and tried to run. He cut a ridiculous figure making the effort, stumbling over his own feet. Nall brought him down with a rugger tackle, though there was no need for such extravagance. He could have followed Tandy at a walk and held him by his sleeve.

'You don't want resisting arrest on your sheet, too, do you, mate?'

'Why can't you buggers leave me alone?'

There were tears not far behind Tandy's voice, tears not very far behind his solemn, idiotic eyes.

'Because you're a bloody lard-head, that's why, Tandy. Because you crack on you know something, and then you won't bloody tell us.'

Nall saw Tandy's jaw tighten. The little man was remembering his principles.

'I'll tell you what I've a good mind to do, Tandy. I've a good mind to let you go again. I've not set eyes on you this afternoon, that's what I haven't. Because I'm supposed to be here for your bloody benefit, that's what I'm supposed to be here for.'

Tandy looked at him with owl-like lack of understanding.

'I suppose you think that was a clever bit of escapology, up in Brackdale? It didn't cross your hen-piss brain that a lot of people were going to a lot of trouble to give you the chance to get away?'

Tandy continued to look at him with mournful stupidity.

'Why do you think they were so keen to let you go, Tandy?'

Tandy looked as if he was not going to reply, but he spoke at last.

'Because they'd no right bloody holding me, that's why.'

'No right? Who the hell's bothered by what's right? You've been let go, Tandy, to draw somebody's fire. Because the word's gone round in no time that you're at large—just when you were on the verge of coughing. So you can bet there's somebody else roaming the countryside this afternoon who means to get you. Somebody who's not going to give you a second chance to tell us his name. And I'm supposed to be your bodyguard, piss-hooking about like a Boy Scout in the undergrowth. I should bloody cocoa. I haven't seen you, Tandy. Piss off! Scapa! Go up the hill. Go down the hill. See if you can find a way out through those trees. You were in the army, weren't you? You know the feeling, don't you—that you never hear the one that gets you? Ta-ta for now, Tandy. Why should I wear myself to a frazzle, trying to save your skin for you?'

Nall turned and walked briskly away.

'Mr What's-your-name—Copper!—don't go! I can't take any more of this.'

The lump in Tandy's throat was beginning to choke him. 'No—bugger you!'

Nall put the mouthpiece of his transmitter to his lips.
'I have it, sir. What Tandy saw when Larner got out of his Lotus and started walking the rest of the way to the Hall was another car coming down. He doesn't know whose car it was, but he saw who was in it: Dyer, Cantrell and Furnival. They stopped and made Larner get in with them.'

CHAPTER 27

'I said I wanted to be able to see to shave in the bottom of this boiler, lad. I couldn't see to find my arse-hole with a sheet of bumf.'

What a Musical Director or Co-ordinating Producer could get away with in the way of personal relationships was as nothing compared with the tolerance of a *chef de cuisine* for his most newly recruited dogsbody.

'You may think you've got all bloody morning, lad. The rest of us haven't. Some bugger will be wanting to eat at midday.'

Admittedly the kitchen was working under pressure. Lord Furnival insisted that they cater for vegans, gastric ulcers and cholesterol-dodgers, as well as for gastronomes at one end and bangers-in-tomato-ketchup addicts at the other.

Peak Low, getting the news early (it would not break in the nationals until tomorrow) had erupted with indignation when they heard what the disciplinary board had done to Freddy Kershaw. Only there were so many versions of it that they could not all have been correct. Kershaw had been dismissed with loss of pension rights; he had been offered a clerical job as civilian attached to the Force—which he had refused outright. He had been sent back to the beat in the least salubrious corner of the county, with two years' extended probation. This he was also said to have declined, thus throwing himself on the labour market.

It had been Kenworthy's idea to ask if there was a vacancy on Cantrell's security staff.

'There's no harm in asking, Freddy. They may jump at you in the hope of your indiscretions.'

But Furnival had not even taken time to consider it. His wisdom of the world was on top and on tap.

'I'm sure we'd be glad of you. By now you probably know more about our weak spots than the Colonel does. But it wouldn't do. They'd all think you were a spy. Go and see Personnel. They'll be able to fix you up with something. Tell them I've said they've got to.'

They had fixed him up at once. Kitchen assistant had been mentioned first as a joke. Kershaw had leaped at it so eagerly that it was a wonder that that alone had not made him suspect.

'I've often wanted to learn top people's cookery,' he said quickly.

'I don't know about top people. You'll find out what goes on at rock bottom. Come back if you can't stand it. We shall be taking on extra box-office staff in another week or two.'

Kitchens were good places to be, not for perks or prime cuts—they watched their shelves with eyes like hawks—but if you wanted to know what was going on. What was being talked about everywhere else had been talked about here first. And there was a constant stream of people in and out from the outside world. This was strictly forbidden—but a determined free-loader of mugs of tea at odd hours is not easily foiled. The kitchen had contemporary equipment, but the premises were old and labyrinthine. There was a very little-used glory-hole that looked as if it had become an alternative unofficial HQ for the drivers of delivery vehicles, construction-site foremen and security patrols between rounds. It was remarkable how little time some of them actually seemed to spend doing rounds. Kershaw knew that if he kept his eyes and ears open, he might well be lucky. He kept himself within earshot of this No. 4 Store.

It was not always easy to be sure that all he heard and saw meant what it seemed to. Towards the middle of his first afternoon there was quite obviously a distribution of funds going on in the glory-hole, with security precautions extraordinary, including lookout men. He thought at first that this was what Kenworthy had told him to be on the watch for, but a furtively close ear—risking draconian reprisals from the chef—informed him it was no more than the daily visit from a bookie's runner with yesterday's settlements. The key revelation, when it finally came, was casual, accidental, a passing non-event.

It was about half past three in the afternoon, and most of the labour force was off duty. He heard someone go into the glory-hole and then, finding no one there, come out into the main kitchen, deserted except for Kershaw, who was at that moment bent over the potato-peeling machine, which had been playing him up since he had been introduced to it that morning. It was perpetually getting itself clogged with scrapings, had constantly to be stopped and partially dismantled. This was what Kershaw was doing at this instant, so he had his back to the newcomer, and since he was in kitchen overalls, the man mistook him for someone else.

'The clots have left it too late. Too much bloody talking.'

Kershaw had the presence of mind to reply with a grunt that could not be recognized as anybody's voice.

'We could only put the frighteners on him, get cracking before he had time to think. Now it looks as if the fuzz are moving in now, so that's where I get off. Is there any char going?'

Kershaw wondered how much longer he could keep himself bent over the machine. But the point was academic. The man had come closer, and without seeing Kershaw's face realized that he had made a mistake.

'Sorry, mate. Thought you were Dave. Who the hell are you, anyway?'

Kershaw stood up. The man was one of Cantrell's guards. He did not know Kershaw.

'Can't help you, I'm sorry,' Kershaw said. 'I'm new here. Not up with the gossip yet. There's char in the urn.'

So what? The frighteners? On whom? Someone on whom they had to get him worried before he had the chance to think. It had to be Cantrell. Blackmail: a conspiracy—some of Cantrell's men, and maybe others in the know. They could only scare Cantrell, could only bluff: Kershaw was not up to date about events: it was only this morning that strange goings-on between Cantrell and his men had been reported. They couldn't act now, it seemed. They'd left it too late. Because the fuzz were moving in. And some of them, at least, didn't want to be involved with the fuzz. Kershaw did not understand it, but he knew that it was an item that had to be got back to HQ as rapidly as possible. And since he was banned from any kind of communication with Gleed, that meant Kenworthy.

The guard helped himself to tea and talked on, grumbling about conditions of work in this place—no doubt a displacement activity to try to cover up his gaffe. As soon as he had gone, Kershaw left the potato-peeler dismantled and walked out into the grounds, wondering where to find Kenworthy.

Kenworthy was nowhere in sight. Why should he be? But up against the balustrade of a folly terrace on the west side of the Hall, Kershaw did see someone he knew. And it was a shock to him.

Sitting together on a bench, as if they were close friends, were Joan Culver and Julian Harper—Joan looking her usual health-poster self—and actually smiling. And Harpur was smiling too—not broadly, but not his normal, surly, private-world introvert self.

Yet it was only a day or two ago that he had hidden on

the stage-set with the sole purpose of scaring the daylight out of Joan.

CHAPTER 28

Gleed sat at his desk and wished that tangential aggro would stop coming for just ten minutes.

First there had been Nall. It was irrelevant for Nall to argue that he had delivered the goods. It was reasonable to concede that he had, but that was not the point. Nall had branched out independently, in the face of the strongest, least equivocal briefing Gleed had ever given. He could easily have compromised an exercise in which every available erg of manpower had been drawn in, depleting duty-rosters county-wide.

Was there any validity in the argument that but for Nall's initiative they still wouldn't have the key information that Dyer, Cantrell and Furnival had picked up Larner in the middle of the night? Where did that get them, anyway? Picking up a man who had just wrecked his car? Driving him home on a filthy night? That was a far cry to a working suspicion of murder. Of course, Gleed would be interviewing the trio, would play one off against the other. But without something meatier than Tandy's claim to have seen them, he couldn't hope for a breakthrough.

He had let Tandy out—and set the top sleuths of the county on the heels of each of the principals—and what had the principals done? Got together in conference. Probably to rewrite *The Road to Emmaus*.

Gleed needed a round of golf, a country walk, an hour for fallow thought. But within a minute his phone rang. Detective-Constable Kershaw.

Oh, Christ! Did nobody do as he was told?

'Now look, Kershaw—I made it plain that you were not

to contact this office. Anything to pass, you're to do it
through Kenworthy—'

Because it was vital that Kershaw's cover should not be
blown, Gleed had done some hard grafting behind the
scenes, laying his own reputation on the line to plead for
Kershaw to get off with a severe rep—and to have him back
here in the undercover role they had contrived for him.

'I'm sorry, sir—but I thought—'

God protect all Superintendents and their kind from
anybody on their staff who ever indulged in the imitative
conceit of pretending to think.

'I thought—I *think,* sir, that this is it. I can't find Mr
Kenworthy. And I think you need to know this.'

'Tell me, then, and I *shall* know.'

Unfair. No man could be giving of his best when he was
in this sort of temper.

Kershaw told him about the presumed blackmail. Gleed
took it in, but stopped short of praise or enthusiasm. He
knew what Kershaw didn't—the tie-up between this and
the peculiar way in which Cantrell's guards had been treating him.

'And have you any idea what this blackmail might be
about?'

'Up to now, no, sir.'

'Well, tell me this, Kershaw—if there is in fact a conspiracy among the security guards, why should a kitchen-
hand be involved in it? Who is this Dave?'

'I'll work on that, sir.'

'Do. And this time you may contact me direct if you come
up with anything.'

Gleed hung up, and the phone rang again almost as soon
as the receiver hit the cradle. Kenworthy.

'Thought I'd better put you in the picture. Furnival rang
me. Wants me over there pronto.'

'Any idea what for?'

'Apparently the three of them have some sort of statement

to make. They want me to help them to put it together. What it amounts to, I guess, is that they want to make their statement to you through me. I'm to help them to *balance* it: that was the word Furnival used. That way, I suppose, they think they'll be better listened to. Shall I be buggering up your plans if I go through with it?'

'Far from it. I was just about to come over to the Hall myself—but I'll leave the field free for you. You've no idea how long this is going to take?'

'None whatever.'

'I may have to interrupt you. I can't afford to wait for ever. I'll give you a couple of hours. And while I've got you, what do you think Cantrell's guards might find to try to blackmail him with?'

'I don't know—but I'm not short of guesses.'

'Guess on.'

'The night Larner's corpse was unpacked from its crate, someone must have issued an order keeping the patrols away from the theatre at the critical time: the beats must have been re-scheduled. Someone may have drawn his own conclusions. Someone may even have *known*.'

'This is beginning to hang together, Simon. But why should a kitchen hand be involved?'

'Someone who witnessed something? You'd better ask Kershaw. If he doesn't know yet all that goes on in that kitchen, he soon will.'

Jimmy Lindop had parked his car in an unfrequented lane not far from Little Longstone. He did a newspaper crossword and dozed, leaving his radio on. Late in the afternoon he heard a news bulletin. Alfie Tandy's 'escape' was reported in not more than a score of words. Jimmy Lindop laughed. It was not until first dark that he drove away from the spot.

He took a road that would get him back to Peak Low.

*

The conversation between Joan Culver and Julian Harpur lasted some half an hour after Kershaw had seen them. Then they broke up, partly because Joan had caught sight of Kenworthy, who was crossing the lawn that edged the terrace. The goodbye smile to which she treated young Harpur would have delighted Freddy Kershaw's heart if it had been directed at him and Harpur shambled away, his face assuming something of its habitual moroseness as he moved out of her sight.

'Well?' Kenworthy asked.

'Amazing. I had no idea. I hope it isn't going to give me a guilt complex.'

'There's no reason why it should. None of it's your fault.'

'It's sad, too. I mean, his parents are to blame, aren't they?'

'You could say so. But is there any point in trying to apportion blame? Many a boy would have survived parents like the Harpurs. Anyway, thank you for trying.'

'I'm not sure that it will work in the long run. I'm not even sure it's wise.'

'Give it a whirl.'

'I think when he finds out how stupid I am about all matters scientific—'

'Just don't let him get you trying to plot the course of a submarine, that's all.'

'I did learn one thing from him. Lord Furnival's wasn't the only car on the Brackdale road that Saturday night. Good Lord—the amount of time that that boy has spent in nocturnal wandering.'

'Unrest. Whose car?'

'He doesn't know their names. But he says he's seen them often enough on and around the stage.'

CHAPTER 29

There was a sense of doomed decision about the faces of the trio. Lord Furnival made some initial pleasantry, but it was mechanical and brought no reaction from the other two. Cantrell was looking flushed and Dyer melancholy.

'Couldn't tell you much on the phone,' Furnival said. 'But I dare say you'll have worked most of it out for yourself.'

He had offered coffee and cognac, which Kenworthy had not declined. Kenworthy noticed that Dyer was taking no alcohol.

'Obviously Gleed will be along presently.'

'I've held him off for an hour or two.'

'From his point of view, we must be highly suspect. He must know we have all three been disingenuous. We have suppressed vital information—all, I might say, to fend off this demon of adverse publicity. But it creates the wrong impression, and that's why I'd rather you put our case to Gleed in the first instance.'

Furnival opened a drawer in his writing-table and brought out a sheet of notepaper.

'It will help, I am sure, if we get the timings right to begin with.'

Saturday, 3.30 p.m. Phone call received from garage in Buxton: Larner had retrieved his car.

6.15 p.m. Cantrell received phone call: his operators had lost track of Larner in Macclesfield.

10.30 p.m. Phone call received: Larner had arrived with Miss Culver at The Grey Cat Club, and had sung numbers from *Passion*.

Sunday, 12.45 a.m. Phone call received from Grey Cat: Larner had left with Miss Culver.

1.30 a.m. Phone call received from Fräulein Mommsen, speaking from kiosk in Peak Low Square. Excited and barely articulate: believed some outrage intended on Larner's car up Brackdale Hill.

I at once informed Cantrell and Dyer. Cantrell rang his theatre command post to order action squad to Brackdale. Some irregularity in application of duty roster, and unable to make contact.

We set out for Brackdale ourselves, but before we had got further than the end of the Hall drive we heard an obvious car crash. We drove on as fast as was safe, and met Larner coming up towards the Hall on foot.

'At this stage,' Furnival said, 'I prefer to take up the narrative orally.'

'One minute,' Kenworthy said. 'You set out for Brackdale —was there any delay in getting on the move?'

Furnival glanced peevishly at Dyer.

'Not everyone had the same sense of urgency. One of us insisted on changing his shoes. And couldn't find the pair he wanted.'

'So how much delay?'

'Five minutes?'

'During which time Detective-Constable Kershaw was running up Brackdale Hill. Sorry to interrupt.'

Furnival had not liked breaking his flow, but he clearly had second thoughts about letting his impatience show too obviously.

'Larner was dazed, but in control of himself—shaken, but not in shock, as far as we could see. The truth is, I don't think he had enough imagination to appreciate what a narrow escape he had had. We got him into the car.'

'You did not think of going down to the scene of the crash?'

Furnival looked uneasy.

'All we thought of was giving him any attention he might need.'

'Did you ask him whether he had had anyone in the car with him?'

'I'm sure one of us must have done.'

'Or were you so glad to have got your own man out of trouble that nothing else mattered?'

Kenworthy in abrasive mood was a phenomenon that Furnival had not met before, and it went against the grain to be spoken to like this.

'I don't care for your attitude, Kenworthy. I'm telling you the truth.'

'And I can understand why you haven't told it before. It sounds pretty thin to me.'

'That is an unhelpful remark.'

'It was meant to be helpful. I'm trying to see things as they will appear to Gleed. So what did you do with Larner? Put him to bed?'

'Not immediately. Brought him back here—to this room. Gave him a drink. Got him to tell us as well as he could what had happened.'

'And how well could he tell you?'

'As I've said, he was somewhat dazed. But he was able to give a coherent account of himself, and I'm afraid, from then on we didn't exactly treat him as needing intensive care. I repeat: there were no obvious symptoms of shock, and I must admit that I didn't consider delayed reaction. We were all too angry. You see, I *am* telling it as it was, Kenworthy.'

'You were angry because his conduct was endangering your show?'

'From our point of view it was a serious matter, Kenworthy. There'd been two or three characteristic businesses with women. In the normal way, show business is pretty permissive, but this *is* a religious play. There'd been a lax scene at rehearsal—Jairus's daughter. There'd been public performances of songs that were still under seal of confidentiality. Then there was the impounded car. He was in breach of contract, and I was sorely tempted to screw it up there and then—which wouldn't have done Dyer any good. I might add, if it hasn't occurred to you, that both insurance and road-tax on the vehicle had run out. What sort of a book could your friends in Traffic have thrown at Jesus Christ, do you think?'

'So you held a kangaroo court?'

'We left him in no doubt as to his future if he did not watch points from then on.'

Furnival remembered to replenish Kenworthy's glass. Kenworthy held up his hand to keep the peg short.

'Yes. This begins to have the ring of truth, Furnival— on balance. But I suggest that a little more expansive truth-telling might add to your credibility.'

'What do you mean by that?'

'I mean other matters about which there has been futile speculation.'

'Such as?'

'Can't you think of any?'

'I don't like being played with, Kenworthy.'

'Mary Magdalene?'

'Not relevant to the main issue.'

'But relevant to the image of a man who is claiming to hide nothing.'

Furnival took a few seconds to recompose himself.

'Not my proudest inspiration, in retrospect. How did you get on to it?'

Kenworthy stared him out. Furnival never was to know whether he was bluffing at that moment or not.

'You have to realize, Kenworthy, that the success of a show like this depends on something more elusive than mere quality. We can buy the finest music, the snappiest lyrics, outstanding costumes, consummate decor, settle the bills for a lavish spectacular. We still need bottoms filling our seats. We need publicity. And publicity sometimes comes by illogical means.'

'Such as the mystery of what is dogging the footsteps of every woman who tries to play the Magdalene?'

'It brought the media to the site and has kept them here daily. The block bookings started shoaling in after Madge Oldroyd's shoes had been nailed to the dressing-room floor.'

'With Ricarda Mommsen primed to write the anonymous letters?'

'A loyal little lady. What happened to her has been the saddest feature of this whole affair.'

'And you put Jimmy Lindop in executive charge of Exercise Magdalene?'

'You haven't missed much, have you, Kenworthy?'

'Which also put Lindop in a position to bugger you about as much as it pleased him to, with his Stalagmites tapes.'

Kenworthy turned in his chair and faced Cantrell squarely.

'And which of you other gentlemen has the urge to confess?'

Cantrell could not hold Kenworthy's eye, but he was clearly going to make a last ditch of it.

'Don't look at me, Kenworthy.'

'No? It seems to me that your night patrols have you over a barrel, Cantrell.'

'I'm afraid you have lost me.'

'This is going to be one of those slow, laborious businesses, is it?'

'Some of them seem to think—'

'What do they seem to think?'

'That there had been some jiggery-pokery with the patrol rosters, the night Larner's body was shifted.'

'And wasn't there?'

'The whole point of security when you haven't enough men on the ground is the random element: unpredictable movements. Don't you see, Kenworthy, it can also work the other way round? The men handling Larner's body must have waited for the rosters to be made known before they chose their time. I must have had a spy in my camp.'

'That story,' Kenworthy said, 'is what is vulgarly called as weak as piss.'

Freddy Kershaw had found his first day of general kitchen duties exhausting. He was ready to drop into bed—if he had enough energy to get himself to his bed—when the *chef de cuisine* waylaid him on his way out.

'Where do you think you're going, Kershaw? You haven't finished by a long chalk. It's Dave's day off.'

'Dave?'

'It's always Dave's job to take the guards their midnight rations—bread, cheese and cocoa. You're standing in for him tonight.'

So that was the connection between bent guards and the kitchen. Dave had seen what he had seen—and had not been slow to get himself dealt in on it.

Kershaw rushed to ring Gleed.

'Piss poor,' Kenworthy said to Cantrell. 'And may I save you the embarrassment of your next line of defence. The changes in rostering were not, repeat not, a coincidence.'

He turned to Furnival.

'I'm sorry, your lordship, but the Colonel's intransigence looks likely to catapult you all back into it. I was beginning to think you might possibly be in the clear.'

'For God's sake, Cantrell—' Furnival said.

'So how long did you spend kangarooing Wayne Larner?'

'Three-quarters of an hour, give or take.'

'And then?'

'Sent him off to his bed with an outsize flea buzzing in his ear.'

'Piss poor,' Kenworthy said again. 'But then, true stories sometimes are.'

It was at this juncture that Gleed arrived.

CHAPTER 30

Gleed caught Kenworthy's eye, querying. How much could one professional man convey to another without speech? There had been relatively little talk between the pair about this case, but their minds were trained along the same tracks.

Gleed gave Kenworthy the go-ahead. *Go on talking,* his eyes were saying. *I'll pick it up when I'm ready.*

'These gentlemen,' Kenworthy said, indicating Furnival and Dyer, 'are going to extract the chestnut for us. Because up to a few minutes ago, they were beginning to look as if they were in the clear. Now Cantrell has buggered things up for them. So shall we leave it to them to deal with him?'

It was doubtful whether even Gleed could put the correct interpretation on a hint as obscure as that.

'Let me put it this way,' Kenworthy said. 'Julian Harpur knows that there were two other men out in a car while these three were picking up Larner. I don't have to tell you, do I? Hajek and Szolnok. Hajek and Szolnok working *together,* gentlemen. I find that significant, don't you?'

There was still nothing forthcoming. Then Gleed spoke, suddenly, in a tone of imperative finality, such as none of them had ever heard him use before.

'Well, Cantrell?'

Cantrell looked as if he was not quite sure whether his

voice was going to respond to his volition. He straightened himself in his chair, as if calling on some military mystique that had stood him in good stead in the past.

'I'm sorry,' he said, 'and I'm afraid I'm going to disappoint you. I was hoping that this wasn't going to come to light, because in all honesty, none of us wants this sort of publicity—'

'Get on,' Gleed said.

'The night when you claim Larner's body was unpacked from its crate, I was approached by Hajek to keep my patrols away from the theatre between two and three-thirty a.m. He was going to try out for himself some stage-lighting scheme that the electricians hadn't got right since rehearsals had started. He'd reached the stage of exasperation in which he was going to make his own experiments at the switchboard and he didn't want any interference.'

'And you believed that story?'

'I'd no reason not to. I'd not been here long before I gave up trying to account for the way these theatrical people organize their lives.'

'Was there evidence that any experiment with lighting effects actually took place? Was there any aura of light over the theatre?'

Cantrell did not know. No one had reported anything. They had not, after all, been checking on Hajek.

'It doesn't make any difference anyway, as far as you are concerned,' Gleed said. 'All right, Kenworthy. There's no need for you to stay. I'm sure you're ready for bed.'

As he undressed, Kenworthy looked out of his window across the parkland. The moon was past its full, and the lines of the theatre looked like marble rather than concrete behind the trees. Pity about the *Passion*. It had had its possibilities.

The show must go on.

That had been Furnival's standby, first thing the next morning. For three weeks, he managed to keep rehearsals going, with his associate producer and musical director doing their best to exploit the flair of Hajek and Szolnok. The new Mary Magdalene, an uncontroversial singer, signed her contract. So did a new—and unimpeachable—Jesus Christ. But everyone knew that they were failing. It was ironical that Furnival had spoken of the illogicality of publicity. Somehow the Press got hold of the truth about the Mary Magdalene pranks. The Mothers' Union withdrew their bookings and that started an avalanche. Agencies and hoteliers rushed to reduce their commitments. Furnival found himself with cash-flow problems. His bankers got cold feet. A month after the arrests he gave in and closed down the show, making brave promises about another year that no one believed.

What happened between Gleed and the Central Europeans took place behind closed doors and was never made public. There is an inevitable drill when two men are being investigated for the same offence, and it is particularly applicable when they hate each other's guts. They are kept apart and talked to separately, and hints are dropped to each that the other is betraying him. The more intelligent they are, the less ready are they to believe this, but solitude and fear breed carelessness. First one, then the other, begins to give away vital detail. Patiently, the interrogating officers piece together the puzzle.

A final picture emerged. Among the hundreds involved in the *Passion,* none stood to lose as much by failure as Hajek and Szolnok. Neither had ever been associated with a failure and what hung in the balance was their next commitment after this. If the *Passion* ended up in chaos, both of them were going to drop their fee on their next commission. The *Passion* was going to fail—and it was going to fail because of Wayne Larner: not on account of his moral aberrations, though they would not help—but because he was æsthetically incompetent for the role he was playing. Hajek and Szolnok had therefore sunk their differences for long enough to agree that Larner had to be edged out of the production while there was still time for him to be replaced.

They met on the Saturday night to draw up their plans, which at this stage amounted to no more than a concerted démarche in front of Furnival. They had a meal together at a quiet hotel on the Sheffield edge of the Peak, and it was on their way back, at the top of Brackdale Hill, that they caught sight of Ricarda Mommsen. They stopped to offer her a lift, but in spite of the hour and the rain, she declined —not, however, before she had tried to tell them an unintelligible and hysterical story. They gathered that Larner had been embarking on new scandal, and that some sort of attack against him was planned. They did not know whether to believe this. They thought the Mommsen girl was mad: but then half the personnel of the *Passion* thought that of the other half. They decided not to go to bed yet, to retire to Hajek's room, whose window commanded a good view of the Hall drive, and whose door was close to Furnival's.

So they knew when Furnival, Dyer and Cantrell came back with Larner. They knew how long he was closeted with them, and they knew when he finally came out of the apartment.

He came in hangdog fashion along the corridor and they did not fall in on either side of him until he was alongside Hajek's door. He was in a confused condition and his attempts to struggle stood little chance against a waist-lock that Szolnok had learned some time in his troubled Central European youth. If any sound of the brief scuffle carried to any of the adjacent rooms, it brought out no curious eyes. Men—and women—perambulating clumsily at night did not rank as news in the Hall.

After a few minutes in Hajek's room, Larner made a bid to escape, whereupon violence simply began to happen. Larner struck wildly about him, and the other two warded blows off with whatever came to hand. A heavy-based table-lamp entered the fray, and so did a wooden stool. Larner's skull was fractured and Hajek and Szolnok had to prolong their alliance.

The moment of highest risk was getting the body out of Hajek's room. But it had to be done, and once they moved, they moved quickly. For seconds they listened for any potential intruder, heard none and transported Larner upright between them, an old hooded anorak of Hajek's over his head, as if they were manhandling a drunk. There was a complex of stables and outhouses fifty yards from the main building which had been used as a builder's yard in the early days, and was now a general dumping ground. Among the debris was a collection of crates and tea-chests containing some of the original stage-set models: Furnival had the idea that they might one day be used in a production museum in an annexe to the theatre. Larner went into an empty crate labelled to contain the walls of Jerusalem. It was collected a couple of days later: crates were always coming and going about the site. The arrangements to have Larner shunted about and finally delivered were complex but not unmanageable. And both Hajek and Szolnok were ready to swear on oath that Cantrell—who had always detested Larner—had known perfectly well why he was being asked to alter the patrol schedules—

In court their counsel denied that their statements had ever been made. He very nearly got them acquitted, suggesting that Larner was almost dead through shock when they found him dazed in the corridor and took him to Hajek's room for first aid. But he had struggled as a drowning man will fight his rescuer, and had been accidentally killed while they were trying to restrain him for his own sake. Convicted of manslaughter, they were both sent to prison.

No charge was preferred against Cantrell, the DPP ruling that there was no material case strong enough to stand up. But the most interesting court appearance was that of Alfred Tandy, who had produced so many changes of statement in custody that they hardly seemed to apply to the same set of circumstances. In spite of this, a seemingly unanswerable charge of attempted murder was brought, backed up by a criminal damage offence. No one doubted his guilt, but the jury, after being out for a day and a half, brought in one of those verdicts that are officially described as *perverse*. 'These twelve gentlemen, in their wisdom—' the judge began acidly as he pronounced Alfie a free man. He did not add the common rider that Alfie left the court without stain on his character.

'I don't get it,' Freddy Kershaw said. 'It seems to me you were running every risk of making things worse.'

'There was that possibility. Kenworthy warned me of that when he suggested I contacted Julian.'

They were eating out—at a Good Food Guide recommendation, high on a ridge overlooking a sweep of open landscape. Joan Culver had been explaining why Kenworthy had persuaded her to go out of her way to talk to Julian Harpur. It had been just after he had given her a fright from the wings when they had been rehearsing the dawn visit to the Sepulchre.

'So he had a crush on you from a distance. And the cure for that was to give him the chance to get to know you— I'd think you were simply encouraging him to go on making an even bigger nuisance of himself.'

'Well, it worked the other way—as Kenworthy said it often does. Freddy—a young man's crush on an older woman is a very sad thing, especially when it's a young man who's labouring under all kinds of other difficulties. But sometimes it works to let the sufferer see how normal his idol is. I felt responsible, Freddy. It was because of me that

he was doing all that mooning about. It was because I was
out with Wayne Larner that he was wandering about up
Brackdale—waiting to see Wayne drive home, wondering
if I'd still be with him.'

'And two chats with you cured him?'

'Not *cured*. How can you cure a boy like Julian Harpur?
But it settled him down in some way—even his mother
admits that. And now, if you don't mind, can we talk about
something nearer home? This place they are moving you to,
Freddy—'

'Ilkeston. Gleed says that's where the action is. A good
place, he says, for a young man with his way to make.'

'You'll get time off, though, won't you—week-ends and
so forth?'

'So that I can have the chance to come and see how
normal you are?'

'I am open to investigation.'

She told herself that she did not know whether she was
in love with Freddy Kershaw or not. But she liked him and
was going to miss him. She did not want to let herself be
influenced by the fact that he would provide a very ready
escape from Peak Low. She had an idea, too, that it would
be very different with Freddy from the way it had been with
the man in Llandudno.

There were, in fact, any number of things that she was
going to allow herself to find out.

When Jimmy Lindop drove away from Little Longstone, he
was almost neurotic about being followed. Twice he slowed
down to a crawl to compel headlamps to overtake him. He
had an appointment tonight that he did not propose to
sacrifice to anyone's need to tidy up administratively after
a mere business of murder.

Although for several miles he had been heading in the
direction of Peak Low, he turned off and drove over exposed
country towards Castleton. At The Grey Cat, The Deviants

were already setting up shop. Lindop started straight in on testing their microphones.

'If anyone asks for *I walked the streets* tonight, you can give it them. Furnival and Co. have other things to worry about than copyright.'

Nall drew air down into his gullet and cracked out a best-ever belch. Old Culver grinned: he had had The Devonshire Arms to himself until the policemen came in.

'Aye,' Sergeant Wardle said. 'The buggers have gone. And I finish in September.'

'Are you staying in Peak Low?'

'The house next door's come on the market and I've put a deposit on it. Mind you, it's going to seem a bit queer at first, seeing things from a different angle.'

The open-air theatre also came on the market. Several times the estate agent's 'Negotiating' sticker appeared over the billboard—but transactions seemed doomed to fall through. Finally, a builder's merchant came in as a squatter, and the auditorium was filled with baths, chimneypots and stacks of scaffolding, the seating having been sold off as a job lot by his lordship's liquidators.

By the second summer after the one which almost saw the *Passion*, the broken windows of the box office had been boarded over. Nettles flourished backstage, and the Parish Council were worried about the danger to children playing on the premises, since two winters' frosts had wrought havoc with the concrete and one corner-stone had already fallen to the ground.